Sworn Before Cranes

SWORN BEFORE CRANES

STORIES BY

MERRILL GILFILLAN

ORION BOOKS

NEW YORK

COPYRIGHT © 1994 BY MERRILL GILFILLAN
ALL RIGHTS RESERVED. NO PART OF THIS BOOK MAY BE REPRODUCED
OR TRANSMITTED IN ANY FORM OR BY ANY MEANS, ELECTRONIC OR
MECHANICAL, INCLUDING PHOTOCOPYING, RECORDING, OR BY ANY
INFORMATION STORAGE AND RETRIEVAL SYSTEM, WITHOUT PERMISSION
IN WRITING FROM THE PUBLISHER.
PUBLISHED BY ORION BOOKS, A DIVISION OF CROWN PUBLISHERS, INC.
201 EAST 50TH STREET, NEW YORK, NEW YORK 10022.
MEMBER OF THE CROWN PUBLISHING GROUP.
RANDOM HOUSE, INC. NEW YORK, TORONTO,
LONDON, SYDNEY, AUCKLAND
ORION AND COLOPHON ARE TRADEMARKS OF CROWN PUBLISHERS, INC.
MANUFACTURED IN THE UNITED STATES OF AMERICA
DESIGN BY JAMIE POTENBERG AND STACY FELDMANN

LIBRARY OF CONGRESS CATALOGING-IN-PUBLICATION DATA
GILFILLAN, MERRILL
SWORN BEFORE CRANES : STORIES / BY MERRILL GILFILLAN.—
1ST ED.
P. CM.
1. GREAT PLAINS—FICTION. I. TITLE.
[PS3557.I3447S85 1994]
813'.54—DC20 93-38694
CIP

ISBN 0-517-59739-X

10 9 8 7 6 5 4 3 2 1
FIRST EDITION

TO MY MOTHER AND FATHER

CONTENTS

SWORN BEFORE CRANES

ALL HEART

THEY always took the back way into Rapid City, if the weather allowed, so that Kabere could see the Indians. Magbar drove her new car and her three brothers always found the same seats: Kaleab beside her—he was nearest her in age—and Asmelash behind her, lost in adolescent squint-thought, with Kabere at the right rear window, his quick eyes snapping it all in like a cat at cream.

They drove east from Flicker a few miles and then cut north on the dirt road, along the best of the Flicker River Valley with its pale bluffs and cedar frettings. Then they were into the Indian country, and Kabere grew more intensely silent and leaned closer to the window and watched each Indian home intently and carefully considered each of those evocative, two-track, white gumbo roads disappearing lazily over the short-grass hills.

They were children of a late, prominent Ethiopian family. Their father had been a quiet well-read man, the governor of a remote Ethiopian province when the political williwaw blew. Then all the children fled to America and eventually, through a network of benefactors and friends, west to the prairie town of Flicker, where they began their American studies at the small red-brick college on the hill. They lived together in a rented house with Magbar smiling at the helm. She was twenty-five, bright, gracious, and long-betrothed, all her pecan-tinted skin, to an Ethiopian boy named Neaman, who was finishing his university education in New York.

Their first Flicker winter was lonely despite their neat and able English. Every two weeks they drove the one hundred miles to Rapid City for shopping, for daily things they could have found in Flicker, but especially for whole, fresh spices at the big food store: spices, especially, for *watt*.

Magbar could easily have laid in enough seasoning for six months, but that was not the idea. The Saturday trip was the thing, the outing through the new landscape, the larger city with its stir and its circling traffic. And then, back home in the early darkness, the steaming trencher of *watt*, the spicy ground-beef dish they had known forever, that made the house smell right and the dreams apricot-colored and breezy.

The boy Kabere, seventeen, had been taken with the western Indians since childhood, taken in the antipodal daydream way that old-world boy children have been taken for a century and a half in London, Paris, Dusseldorf, Dublin, and certain sectors of Addis Ababa. At the age of nine he spent long windowside afternoons gazing at picture books full of free-flowing, war-bonneted men and idyllic tipi villages pitched along sumptuous valleys. He gathered cast-off feathers from city streets, tying them carefully to a tall, peeled willow wand leaning in a corner of his room, and struck alert aquiline poses as he crested hills in the neighborhood park.

Kabere and the youngest brother, Asmelash, were the last to arrive in Flicker. During his first months there, as spring crept in, Kabere took regular, shy drives in the area, carefully visiting the small museums and historic points within a twenty-five-mile radius of his home. He would stop some days as he walked the streets of Flicker and look up at the clouds and think: "These are the sort of clouds the wild Indians lived under, saw from their ponies."

One June day as Kabere was leaving town with his little camera, he saw a broken old man on a single crutch thumbing a ride at the city limits: A Sioux man, the boy said. He stopped and backed up and the man crawled in and said a short hello.

As he drove, Kabere sneaked glimpses of his silent rider: his dark, weathered face, a nose like a windfall pear, large hands that looked as though they had been run over and over and over again. The man had a fast and acrid odor to him. He breathed slowly and deeply as though he were sound asleep and very wise, with his splayed hands interlocked on the bandaged crutch handle.

Three miles from town, the man pointed at a group of house trailers and said, "I get out here." Kabere pulled off the highway at the gravel entrance beside a fleet of mailboxes. The old man leaned in before he shut the door, his dewlap swaying, to thank the boy thoroughly for the ride. That night in bed Kabere told Asmelash in a low voice that he had met an Indian.

A week later Kabere saw the old man standing on a down-

town corner. When the boy had run his errand and returned
the man was still there, standing heavily with a carton of cigarettes tucked under one arm. Kabere slowed, then timidly
approached and said hello.

The old man slowly shifted his eyes to take in the boy's
face.

"I gave you a ride last week, out east from town," Kabere
said softly.

"Yes."

"Do you live in those trailer houses?" Kabere asked.

"I live in number seven, way in back."

"Perhaps I will visit you one day, if that is alright."

The old man looked at the boy's face again. "Sure, that's
alright."

Two days later, a Saturday when the car was available, Kabere drove to the trailer park late in the afternoon. He had
his camera in his pocket. He drove slowly among the dozen
ramshackle trailers until he spotted number seven. He
knocked at the ramshackle door. No reply. He got back in
the car to wait.

By the next trailer a car and a pickup truck were parked.
They were full of luggage and household goods. Both carried Missouri license plates. Now and then a man came out
to carry something inside. Behind the trailer a young boy sat
rocking trancelike in a chain swing and wailing like a howler
monkey.

Kabere sat there almost an hour. Cars and trucks came and
went noisily. All the trailer people were blond and fat. An
Ethiopian boy had never seen so many fat people in all his
life. He wondered if they would be fat even if they were
starved, if they would stay fat on the outside and starve up

in the center. Kabere from his car could hear kitchen crashings and toilet flushings. He smelled cooking food. The vague sounds of either people copulating or maybe a puppy locked in a bathroom. The day began to dim.

Then a pickup stopped by the mailboxes and Kabere saw the old man climb from the passenger side, lean in to thank the driver, and come limping down the gravel lane.

Kabere got out and hailed him as he neared the trailer. The old man looked and waved the boy inside. Kabere stood just inside the door while the man took off his coat and hat and leaned his crutch in a corner and replaced it with a cane. The man smelled of liquor. The trailer smelled like the man. From a paper bag he slid a can of corned beef hash and a can of cheap sardines and a bottle of muscatel.

"What are you up to?" he asked the boy.

"I wanted to come and visit you," Kabere said. Then, after a moment: "I am interested in the Indians."

"Hunh," the old man grunted as he emptied an ashtray into the garbage sack. "Hunh. Sometimes the Indians treat me right and sometimes they don't." He talked through a fog as he fiddled with his cigarettes and fumbled to light lamps.

"It's hard to say about that. . . . They don't go for me much. I've been up here thirty-five years and I've had good and bad from the Indians. I don't know. I was born in Nogales, Mexico. Came up here in 1951. I still speak pretty good Spanish, too."

Kabere looked away from the old man and caught his own reflection in a window glass. He watched it for a short moment, tall and thin like a crooked stick.

The old man had settled onto a ratty sofa and had opened the muscatel. After a pull he told Kabere the patchwork tale of a professional football career. He had been pretty good. He smoked and drank and stretched the story out. Quarterback with the Green Bay Packers after the war. Made pretty good money. Never quite broke beyond second string.

"Vanceneas is my name. Vanceneas—that's a Spanish name. I'm in the football books."

Kabere left the trailer after a half hour and climbed into his sister's car. There were lights on in nearly all the trailers now, harsh, strident lights, and scattered music. He drove slowly west toward town. The latter sunset was sending shafts of unearthly orange up from behind the pine ridge.

The boy was disappointed, but not cowed. He had made a small mistake his first time, that's all. A small, dignified mistake. No one would ever know about it. The Mexican himself didn't even know about it. And there would be *watt* tonight.

ON SLEEP CREEK

SATURDAY mornings just after daybreak in the Flicker River country, on one of the faint gravel roads threading the gumbo hills and the buttes, a dilapidated green and yellow school bus crawls at a walker's pace before a halfhearted cloud of blond dust. Being the largest, clumsiest thing by far to travel these byways, its oversized, gaudy stripes are recognized from miles away by local rural people, who have known it for years and call it "the Caterpillar."

The bus is driven by an elderly man, tall and stout, wearing thick spectacles and a black cowboy hat. His wife sits behind him in the single remaining passenger seat. The rest of the vehicle is stowed with odds and ends spilling from cardboard boxes and hanging from the sidewalls. There is a portable hanger-rack of dresses, a dolly full of winter coats and a wooden bin on skate wheels crammed with toys, and a bit of everything littered about the floor.

Each Saturday the old trader and his crusty wife drive their load of secondhand goods up into Indian country to set up in some public place. There, in a parking lot or a wide spot in the road, they deploy their wares in the sunshine and sell and trade for half a day, then load up and move to another village. It is a desultory, pre-burgher commerce old as dice. One week they show up on White Clay Creek at the edge of a box elder grove and later down at Slim Buttes. The next week they rattle into Red Shirt, almost under the shadow of the Black Hills, and then into Oglala for the afternoon, where the rack of dresses rocks brightly in the wind. Another Saturday they start before daylight and make the long drive to Potato Creek and Lost Dog and the staggeringly vast Eagle Nest Butte country, and crawl and grind around that top-of-the-world terrain for a long day.

It is pleasant to see them moving along far off across the hills, plying their low-gear trade. They are remnants, perhaps the final descendants of the wandering pedlars, the reddlemen and the liniment hawkers and the itinerant scissor-sharpeners of yore. The old bus moves at a sane pace through sane country, all the lofty plain from Beaver Creek to the Badlands: the miles of sinewy grassland; ranges of huge columnar cottonwoods lining the streams (the cottonwoods are crucial, always and actively there, like whiskey in the Irish stories); and above, presiding, the dark, pine-netted hills and fragrant ridges with their chalky, wind-gnawed cliffs that shine for many miles. Indian land: unharassed, knowing land, rarely gashed or uprooted. And in the simplest of transactions it seems to reciprocate: as a theater for human life and drama, it cradles, resonates, consoles. . . .

❧

IN THE old days, the green and yellow bus often visited a fellow (though considerably more anchored) specimen of the tradework, a root-hog outpost on the northern edge of the Sioux lands. That was where the bus trader drank a cup of coffee and swapped a box of hair nets for a coil of heavy-gauge wire, then spat on the ground and turned the Caterpillar back toward Flicker.

The trading post was a jerryrigged place built of rough slab lumber. It stood on the flats on the east side of Sleep Creek a few miles above its juncture with the Cheyenne River. The place still functions today in a diluted after-thought sort of way. Rusty gasoline pumps stand in front and old pale tumbleweeds pile high on the west wall. A weathered sign above the door reads "Sleep Creek Merchandise" and a smaller much-abused handmade one on the porch railing reads "Used Cow Parts" and shimmies nervously in the steady Sleep Creek wind.

The white-bearded man who runs the place today lives in two dark rooms in the rear of the building. During summer months when there is still a certain amount of tourist traffic on the Sleep Creek road, he opens the store regularly, selling ice and beer and candy and the occasional souvenir; a pretty mule deer antler or a fossil from the Badlands. Badger hides and dusty snakeskins hang on the walls. The old man leans heavily on the thick glass case and recites oft-rehearsed wild-west talk for touring easterners, the perpetual cold sore on his lower lip filling periodically, well-like, with thin blood to overflowing, when he daubs it with a gory handkerchief.

The other half-dozen homes in the one-time village, some of them sizeable frame houses, are empty and broken. The tiny post office is boarded up, the slab-lumber saloon locked and full of spiders. But in the years following the Second World War Sleep Creek was doing well on the tourist trade.

Its level, handsome valley was a natural approach to the Black Hills in those days, before the superhighways. A daily train went through. Things happened there.

On a good day back then, the owner, a man named Frankie, would have his hands full. He had a hired boy to pump the gasoline while he himself handled the steady flow of tourists, on the one hand, and vicinity Sioux on the other. To the former he sold many pounds of refreshments and groceries, keepsakes and trinket beadwork. To the Sioux he provided kitchen utensils, lunch pails, lamps, Jell-O molds, Czechoslovakian seed beads, dog collars, dolls, dinner plates, tweezers, antelope hooves, plastic wreaths, children's sunglasses, penny ashtrays, deer tails, cascades of rubber ivy, salt-and-pepper sets, car jacks, napkin holders, and fry pans. He lived alone in a nice house off behind the store and found his fun in Rapid City to the north.

But first and foremost, Frankie was a snake-and-bone man, and proud of it. Those were the cargoes that distinguished him from ordinary merchants like the Caterpillar man. Frankie was a plump, unambitious, mercantile man with flighty brown eyes that tended toward warmth and good humor, then shied away, jumped to skyline. They gave him an unfastened quality that was heightened by his habit of continuously hoisting his blue jeans and fiddling with his belt. He came across one day as a good, odd man and the next as mercurial and possibly mean.

He was proud of the oddball slot of his main commodities, the snakes and the bones. He collected two and three hundred rattlesnakes a summer, hunting the den sites and the prairie dog towns with a buddy or two, and sold them to the Reptile Gardens up in Rapid City. He loved taking a visitor into the backyard building he called his "bone shed" and rummaging through the man-high tangle of old elk and deer antlers, fossilized buffalo skulls, longhorn racks, piles of antelope horns and steer femurs. Tourists took them home to hang above their doorways or to set out in the petunia patch. Frankie would whistle and mutter as he bent and tugged in the pile. "I must have a thousand dollars worth of elk in here, my friend."

And more than that he loved escorting tourist families into the snake room, a catchall compartment just off the main store. There he would lead them to a heavy table supporting three large fish tanks full of seething, pent-up rattlers and an occasional prime bullsnake. Frankie would stand nonchalantly to one side while the family uneasily admired his stock and asked him the same daily questions. To a pretty woman he would say with a twitching straight face, "There's a nice little bullsnake right there. Reach in and pick him up. Go on."

All summer long he did that. Showed the bones, showed the snakes and rapped on the tank to make them churn and sizzle. Stood, hitching his trousers, behind the counter with a loaded double-barreled 20 gauge beneath it. Late mornings, the train rocked up the valley beyond the highway and Frankie bent his head an inch or two to watch it go by. And toward noon, as he was dusting off and bagging a coyote hide or a painted-up calf pelvis for a tourist, he saw the Slows come striding into town, right on time: four lank middle-aged men approaching down the railroad tracks in stiff single file, in the halting rhythm of tie-walkers. Opposite the store they left the tracks and marched, without breaking figure, across the highway and into the little town.

For three decades a woman rancher some miles downstream recruited and hired slow men and boys; befriended,
housed, and fed them in exchange for ranch work. She began
the practice shortly after being widowed, bringing in a pair
of slow-learning brothers from a nearby shattered family and
getting them through high school and even into the army.
She did it out of Christian sentiment and practical need. She
was straight with and good to them, and to the half-dozens
who followed over the years, an ever-changing kaleidoscopic
group of four or five at most, men of varying age and men-
tality from all over the upper plains. They came for a year or
two, or five, and then left for who knows where, and were
replaced. They had a part of the big well-kept ranch house
to themselves. She fed them well and left them alone.

One summer late in life Anna knew she had a winning
combination: four men who had been with her a long time.
They were dependable and got along well and she had come
to enjoy them like family. So one fey September she made
her will leaving the ranch with guardian provisions to the
foursome, or whoever among them would stay with it. It was
a beautiful spread at the junction of Sleep Creek and the
Cheyenne: the spruce white and green house surrounded by
a flock of white and green outbuildings and a pair of barns,
all situated on a pleasant flat on the leeside of the valley. Her
white-faced cattle roamed up the creek and down and over
into the wide Cheyenne bottoms.

And before too long her "slow boys," as she called them,
owned the place and did just fine. Each had his own shaving
mirror on the kitchen wall. They had four radios stationed in
far corners of the house. They showed up in Sleep Creek
village several times a week, tall and gaunt the four of them,

stalking through in their faded overalls on various errands, always in that stately single file with a body-length between them, cowboy-hatted, poker-faced wanderers stepped down from a haywire Grecian urn. Everyone called them the Slows as a sort of surname. The four men bought chewing gum or cigarettes or groceries and stood quietly in front of the store watching the traffic pass by. The first of each month they visited their benefactress's grave on the edge of town—a heartfelt, rentlike day.

Niels was the best known of the foursome, the most social and the strongest of the group. He wore a wide leather belt on the outside of his overalls, with a heavy bucking-horse buckle. The woman had found him at a mission in Rapid City; he came originally from the Moreau River country up around Maurine. He worked hard and was even enterprising. For some years after his arrival on Sleep Creek he had been a prolific, matter-of-fact rattlesnake catcher, appearing regularly at Frankie's door just after sundown, deeply sunburnt, with a lidded plastic bucket that, if you hushed and leaned over it, emitted a low and steady, sand-gritty sound.

After the woman died, Niels frequented the store more than ever, standing to one side quietly. Other than "Hello, Niels. How's Niels today?" people paid him no mind.

One Friday night eight months after the old woman was buried, Niels walked into the store with a burlap sack. He had found a big snake near the barn that day. Frankie was having a little party. He was sitting at the coffee counter with three floozies from Rapid City and his friend Jake, a skinny man from down the road with inexpensive watery eyes. It was a hot night. They were drinking highballs, hard at it for the weekend.

Frankie came over to meet Niels and took the sack back into the snake room. Niels stood blinking, staring at the dressed-up women in the bright light: brash red lipstick and cool white teeth. Frankie came out and paid Niels for the snake and looked quizzically at the big man's blinking face. Then Niels left and walked off down the dark tracks, past the haystacks and the warping stock chutes and across the trestle bridge toward home.

The next day about noon when Niels appeared across the road, Frankie whistled into the back of the store and one of the floozies hurried out. She peeked from the window on tiptoe, then threw a thin sweater over her shoulders and left the store. She hailed Niels as he cut across the highway. He stood stone still and watched her soberly as she talked, rocking from one high-heeled foot to the other. Cajolery in the cool Saturday air.

And then, just like that, the two walked off. She took him to an abandoned, half-finished house with a ratty sofa and beer trash in it a hundred yards from the road. Frankie and Jake and one of the girls were already there, hidden stocking-footed and smirking in a closet with their peepholes prepared.

❧

IT WAS months before Frankie's occasional rough-hewn insinuations penetrated Niels's quotidian and a nasty glimmering took hold in his mind. It fluttered and guttered, and one day it was all clear as flint.

The revelation was stark but its chemistry was complex for Niels. Once he knew what had happened, he thought about it a good part of his days and weeks, mulled on it at work in the barn and while greasing his clodhoppers and over the favorite supper he cooked for the Slows, a huge mound of mashed rutabagas with fried eggs on top.

It was an intrusion of consequence, he knew that. A year after the woman had taken him to the sofa, he thought of her occasionally and simply. It was a love, the only way he knew what lurked behind that word: a simple, barnyard love. He had *loved* her, his love was once and for all upon her, regardless if she never entered his life again. It was his only private height. Now it was contaminated by the new thing, the shifty leer through fat prairie-dog cheeks. A flushed resentment focused and grew to a pinpoint hatred.

Niels never hinted that he had figured things out. The subject even dropped from Frankie's attention over the next half year. Niels continued to visit the store, and stood longer, even more quietly, off to one side, waiting instinctively for more light, further instructions.

He was there one early August day when the Kentuckians came. A lean dark-haired man and his wife and tongue-tied twelve-year-old boy. They were headed for Wyoming to fish and going up to Mt. Rushmore to see "the faces." Frankie took them in back to see the snake tanks. When they returned the Kentuckian drank a cup of coffee and talked Appalachian snake talk; told about the religious snake handlers moaning and lowing; and how the poor mountain folks and wageless striking coal miners turned to timber rattlers for table meat; how in bad-blood time a sack of snakes might be dumped in an enemy's parked car just to let him know he's thought of.

And three days later, Sunday morning, Niels put in a long day poking around his old haunts with his grimy lidded bucket and his forked pole of ash. He chose only strong, good-sized snakes. He worked steadily the following days, going out each morning and evening when he could spare an hour to hunt the dens and wander sharp-eyed through the big prairie dog town down by the river.

Friday night Niels ate an early supper with his ranchmen—pork chops and rutabagas and fried eggs and apple sauce. Then he left the house. He sat in the near-dark of the small barn. One by one he fished out his best big snakes from the bucket and held them down with his feet and cut off their rattles with his Barlow knife, then dropped them back in. Then he put the lid on and took up the bucket and struck out surely across the stubble field to the tracks.

He walked slowly along the old cinder bed of the railway, thinking about the thing he wanted to do. When he stopped to rest he heard the angry sandpapery stirring in the bucket. He would walk to the edge of town and wait for darkness in the fencerow trees behind Frankie's place.

As he moved along the tracks, thinking all about the thing, he spied a dead pronghorn kid crumpled in the ditch below, thrown there by a thundering truck. Niels stopped and looked and then clambered down the embankment. He stood and gazed at the creature for long seconds while redwings sang around him in the late sun. It was a runt of a critter with giant foggy eyes. It was sad and pretty as a puppy. It lay there numb and finished off with all its bones pulverized like glass in a sack and its tiny tongue lolling out.

This would be better, Niels thought. He bent a little to see the body in the apricot light. Yes, this would be a better thing than snakes in the truck. He set down his bucket and hoisted the dead kid over his shoulder. He carried it to town and into the brushy grove and waited still as a stump under a cottonwood until it was full dark and nobody moved in the half-lit yards and houses. Then he took it quietly across the lot to Frankie's, stood for a moment, and carefully set it up on the porch at the top of the steps—fixed it up facing the door just the way he wanted it, like a spread-eagle voodoo mantis or knock-kneed kamikaze angel, and slipped back into the dark of the trees.

A Photo
of
General Miles

THREE or four times a summer I would pack my knapsack good and full and hike off up Deer Creek for a long day. Up the stream about two miles one leaves the ponderosa hills and gullies and steps forth onto a little-suspected plateau, high and open and powerfully rolling and lush enough with its tiny headwater streams to have the comfortable feel of a northern meadow.

I would hike for an hour across this secretive steppe without seeing a human being; seeing little but the meadow birds flushing up from the tall grass and an occasional edgy horse herd. There was a single minimal dirt road crossing the plateau from east to west. It hooked and sliced and led past a rocky jumble of deteriorating cliff known locally as an old buffalo jump site. A regional entrepreneur took a busload of Japanese tourists there once, but when the first of many rattlesnakes sounded from the scree the visitors stampeded back to the bus and refused to get out until they were back in Billings.

A few minutes beyond this place I arrived at my knoll, from which I could see the Rosebud Mountains to the south and west. I set up my sawed-off easel and lashed down my pad against the jaunty wind and painted or sketched—on clear days the Big Horns were visible still farther south— and ate my lunch of bread and cheese and olives. When I tired of painting the far mountains or the cloud-shadowed swells of the plains below I turned to the plants at my elbow and drew the wild roses or the lovely bunches of delicate June grass with their sharp, plaintive upthrust as of nestlings in a nest.

Then I would pack up my things and give myself a once-over for ticks and walk down over the hill to see Ruben Bear. I happened across his house two summers ago on a day with the easel. It was a small old house, but firm and well patined. It was the only home I knew of on the whole vast plateau.

Ruben was in his sixties, sturdy and quiet, with a quick and nimble grin. He lived there with his wife and often a handful of visiting grandchildren. He still took plenty of deer for the table and his wife put by plenty of cherries and plums. By the end of August there were festoons of sliced, strung squash drying from the porch rafters.

That first day we talked a little in the yard and I showed them my sketches and soon we were drinking coffee around their table. Out the kitchen window I could see, perched on a low rise immediately above the house, a rickety metal fold-ing chair, sitting there alone amid the patchy sagebrush.

As I was saying good-bye in the yard I noticed it again—

standing out against the sky—and said, "That's a good spot somebody has up there."

"Yes," Ruben said. "That's my spot. I go up there with my drum sometimes at night. To sing. Just to entertain myself."

I hadn't seen the photograph that time. That was the next visit, maybe three weeks later. It was a small photograph in an ornate wooden frame, sitting on a chest of drawers. The print was creased and splotchy and showed three Indian men with carbines and a white-haired soldier squinting in a hard sun.

"That one is my grandfather," Ruben said, pointing at one of the long-haired men in calico shirts and moccasins. "He was a scout for General Miles. That picture was taken at Fort Keogh, up on the Yellowstone River."

Ruben and I became friends, in a widely spaced way. I stopped when I could. I would halloo as I entered the yard, or, more likely, Ruben would have heard me coming and, tapping an old contrary vein of wit, burst out the door looking in the opposite direction, scratching his head and saying in a rhetorical stage whisper, "I could swear I heard somebody drive in." They were tonic visits, those hours spent sorting beans or scrubbing melons from the garden with a near-content man of good ear and good eye who when the night was right climbed the little hill to the rickety chair to sing with the stars.

Some days, I saw that the photograph was not in its usual place. Other times it was there, front and center. One afternoon when it was missing I alluded to it as obliquely as I could and Ruben went to the chest and lifted it from a drawer.

He brought it over and sat down and told me about it in one gentle, well-tempered stanza. His family had always been proud of the picture—his grandfather was widely known as a good man, a good father, and a good fighter. Then some years ago when things stirred up on many of the reservations, and Indian peoples began to stand forth more publicly for their ways, some young people began to talk about the grandfathers in the fighting days. They began asking questions and reading the history books and finding out about those days.

Some of them read about those among their people who had helped the white soldiers in their later campaigns, scouted for them against Chief Joseph or the holdout Sioux, located the tired hostile camps and led the soldiers to them.

Those names and those stories spread quickly among the younger generation. The elders had of course known all those stories forever; they knew the grandfathers scouted to avoid the staked-down dry-rot life at the fort. But people began to look at other people and think of what their grandfathers did in the fighting days. People talked and said things and others heard them. It was a difficult time for many families when the good, sleeping past came back bitter and wild-eyed.

So when Ruben looked out his door in those days and saw an unfamiliar car coming down to his house, he would sometimes walk over and put the photo in the drawer with the good tablecloth. Just to avoid some things, some little troubles. He didn't like the thought of people talking about his family in town.

But eventually Ruben himself began to think about the thing. He went back and forth with it, and still did. He summoned those old days and tried to see them, tried to see what that scouting for the white soldiers amounted to a hundred years later—was it such a good thing after all? Some days he thought no, and the picture went into the drawer. Other days he looked again with his good glasses on and said, "Father of my father," and set it on the table beside a chewed-up prayer book and a tumbler of spoons.

From then on, I always stole a glance around the room when I got there, to see how the issue stood that week, to gauge how the ancestral karma ran. It was a detail among many, but I knew it fed the star songs and I simply made a point to notice it as I noticed the direction of the wind through the web of things and the light and lay of the Rosebud range on my way back over the hill.

BLACKBIRDS ON
THE POWDER

EUGENE Bricker moved to Broadus late in life for the penultimate noble reason: a down-to-earth, well-preserved woman with bluish hair who had returned to her family home on Wilbur Street when her husband died and a fierce ground-swell grief drove her from Dubuque.

They met through mutual friends in Denver. Within six months they agreed they should be nearer. Eugene had retired from a theater-seat manufacturing company that had ceilinged and leveled off to leave him (in ironic contrast to his wares) "comfortable." So two years after the war, he followed Mrs. Curtin to Broadus, where a surprisingly deep and well-choreographed passion bloomed and spread like kudzu for almost a decade.

Their affair was for the most part a successful secret, for no real reason, with simple successful rules. Mrs. Curtin would never remarry; she had taken a grief-cast vow on that. They both enjoyed the casual, worryless discretion as a sort of chutney to things.

Eugene took a small house on Trautman Avenue, where he read sleepy western fiction, tended a bed of flowers, and fished the little streams dancing from the Big Horns. He hung deer antlers that he found on his outings along his white picket fence. Mrs. Curtin cooked and canned for the pleasure of it and wrote long sweet letters to the trans-Mississippi. She kept her lawn fine and religiously deep-watered a twelve-foot ash tree to ensure the proper shimmering fall foliage that reminded her of the towering October color along the bluffs above Dubuque.

Winter nights were easy, with the early dark. Eugene would stroll down Trautman Avenue at the edge of town and join her for dinner, slipping in the back door to the kitchen. At midnight he walked home, humming to himself. Summer nights they often met up on the Powderville Road, a little-used dirt track following the river north of town. They found a plentiful grove or a cool sandbar in the Powder and watched scores of sunsets there.

They traveled together often over eight years, motoring about the West from Glacier Park and Jasper to the Dakota Badlands and Estes Park. They drove down to stay at the Don Pratt in Belle Fourche and then on for big steaks in St. Onge. They strolled in straw hats among antique threshing machines convened at Bird City, Kansas, and gazed over Willow Bunch, Saskatchewan, from the handsome alder-skirted hills just south. They danced in Omaha, Portland, and Miles City. They reached amorous heights in Jackson Hole and La Junta that left them speechless as hounds.

When Mrs. Curtin died in 1955, Eugene spent days alone on the slender butte above the cemetery and the old white school, sitting shapelessly amid the sagebrush and staring at the Powder River trees across the valley. He wanted to pound out an endless, stupefying rhythm on some kind of elemental drum. The tall radio antennae on the point above him seemed to gather, intensify, and broadcast his sorrow; that occurred to him after a week up there. Then he sold out and returned to Denver.

❖

ROY turned off the highway onto Cottonwood Street. He hadn't been in Broadus for many years, but he always remembered where to turn. He knew his uncle Eugene's house stood on the corner of Cottonwood and the easternmost street of the town, that it had been pulled down in the midsixties and replaced by a sixty-five-foot mobile home. But Roy felt like stopping anyway. He parked in midblock and got out and stretched. He threw his cigarette on the sidewalk and stepped on it. The sole of his cheap summer shoe always melted a smear when he did that and the butt stuck to it. He scraped it off on the grass and walked down the block.

Roy had visited his uncle just twice in Broadus, when the family was up that way. And Eugene had stopped to see Roy's family on occasion—never with the woman of course. He often brought Roy a gift of six or eight airline liquor bottles—full ones—accumulated on his travels. Roy remembered Eugene as perpetually pulling something interesting to eat from his basement freezer—antelope steaks or elk roasts or dark prairie grouse he roasted on beds of sauerkraut. One night he stuck half a dozen small trout on sticks like hot dogs and cooked them over coals.

Roy was never close to his uncle; lazily fascinated was

more like it. Even now, back in Broadus, he sensed the vague possibility of learning something more about Eugene even though the man was dead two decades.

Roy walked past the homesite. TV prattle blared from the trailer's open windows. He walked on, turning north, up several blocks to the new high school, then cut left. He registered only the old houses that remained from his uncle's day, tight bungalows, most of them. A mustard stucco with white trim and matching garage. A salmon stucco with lavender trim. A tiny white one with lime green trim in a dense grove of poplars. A crumpled tangerine stucco with red ivy above the door and a hot metal roof. Off to the northeast of town he saw the dry, angular buttes above the Powder River where the hard plains jackknifed to the valley.

Roy turned back through town and passed a couple of cafés and a dried-up bar called the Powder River Club, its letters barely legible on the brown stucco wall. He wondered if his uncle ever patronized those places, if anyone in there right now might have known him, hunted or fished with him. He wondered how Eugene had picked this little dusty town. It is all thin as fish skin, tough as cholla, once it's gone.

But Roy wanted to get to Rapid City that night. He circled back to his car and wheeled around to the highway.

On the southeast edge of town, just beyond the river, he stopped at a rest area to use the toilet. When he got back to his car, there was a man leaning against the front fender, preoccupied with a set of headphones.

He looked up as Roy approached. He was a young man, over six feet tall with reddish hair and a rumpled sort of look to him.

"I'm heading back to Chicago and wondered if you could

give me a lift as far as you're going." Roy stopped and stared. "I saw you pull in; I was back under those trees." The man nodded toward a brushy fencerow.

Roy was caught out. He picked up hitchhikers now and then in the hinterlands, on small roads where he could take a good look at them. He was leery of the federal highway hikers nowadays. But he was caught out this time.

"I'm only going to Rapid City," he hedged.

"That's a step in the right direction," the red-headed man said and moved toward the passenger door of the Oldsmobile. The negotiations were closed.

As they pulled onto 212, Roy glanced at his rider close up. His face was long and open with large blue eyes and thick fleshy lips whose weight kept them perpetually open and dry. His light red hair was thin and floated up from his head. He had a wild look, up close, a John Brown sort of look, pushing out through the eyes.

"You're traveling pretty light," Roy said. The man had a brown paper bag and headphones with a small cassette player riding on his belt. A light jacket with a hood.

"I always travel light. I've been out here three weeks, bumming around. Caught a freight train from Chicago to Gillette, Wyoming. I come out every year. Got to get away from the big city."

"Just bum around for a while, huh?"

"That's it. Just air out for a few weeks. Those cities will bag you if they get the chance."

The man lit a cigarette and smoked continuously thereafter as they climbed onto the Powder River highlands, the strong stark hills and far spindly spires and buttes, the pronghorns browsing near the road. The rider observed it all intently, leaning and turning to look in all directions as he talked.

"I don't trust those little dipstick towns, though, I'll tell you that. I just go in for cigarettes or a loaf of bread and that's it.

"They aren't as bad as back East though," the man talked on. "I met an old boy down in Wyoming who had been picked up in Missouri, some dipstick town. Some old lady saw him walking the tracks through town and called the cops. The old man hid in the woods, but they finally got him. Must have had twenty cops and deputies looking for one old coot. All he wanted was to blow on through anyhow.

"Mind if I make a sandwich? I haven't eaten much today." He settled his paper bag between his feet and clawed through its contents. He pulled out half a loaf of bread and was reaching into it when a jet to the south caught his large radar eyes.

"Look at that—fighter jet," he said, freezing with the bread in his hand. "Looks like an F-16 from here." He followed the plane until it disappeared west.

"Know what the first long-range fighter jet was?" he asked Roy and resumed his sandwich building. Roy looked over at him, grunted no. The man had pulled out a jar of Cheez Whiz and a plastic knife.

"P-51 Mustang—tail end of World War II. Had to have them to cover the bomber raids over Germany." He spread the Cheez Whiz on thick.

"Before that the air force was getting creamed over there. April '44: 8th Air Force lost 577 planes over Europe. October '43: big raid on ball-bearing plant in Schweinfurt. Flying from England. Out of 291 heavy bombers sixty went down.

One blow-out after another. Then they dreamed up the P-51 to escort them in."

Roy shifted in his seat and glanced at the man eating his sandwich, sweeping the skyline as he chewed.

"June '44. Operation Pointblank. Saturation bombing in France to soften things up for the Normandy invasion. One and a quarter million tons of bombs on the Germans that year. And 12,000 French and Belgian civilians killed in the Pointblank bombings—12,000 innocent people. How's that grab you?"

The man wiped his lips and drank from a small canteen, lit a cigarette.

"Check this," he went on. "D Day the U.S. bombers coming in over St. Lo to cream the Germans let loose a barrage and catch their own front lines with it: 800 casualties the first time around. 1500 Allied casualties that season from friendly air action. That's what they call it: *friendly action.* Friendly blood and guts I call it."

Roy cleared his throat and cracked his window. "You were in the service?" he asked the man.

"Nope. I just study the stuff. Got into it when I was a little kid. I was born during Dien Bien Phu—that's the only reason I could ever figure out."

Roy slowed to ease around a fresh pronghorn carcass lying in the road. The crows lifted and hovered long enough to let him by.

The hitchhiker rested for a while, scanning the low hills with his radar eyes. Roy chewed a Chiclet and kept the Olds at seventy. After ten minutes the man began to smoke and talk again.

"But I tell you, Japan was where the air force learned

some lessons. Trying to reach Japan from the Marianas. Hard enough just to get those B-29s airborne. Had to take off into the wind from a short runway. Hell, all those pilots knew the Japs beheaded any airman that went down over there. Tried to get up high and go in thataway. First time up there, 30,000 feet, after coming in all the way from the Marianas, bomber fleet hits 150-mile-an-hour winds, bang— couldn't see or do diddly squat for target location. Blew them right on over the whole country before they knew what was happening. Know what that was?"

Roy cleared his throat and shook his head.

"Jet stream. That's how they discovered the jet stream."

Roy saw a feeble river bottom a few miles ahead where it crossed 212. He knew that would be Alzada.

They rolled into the village and Roy slowed for the single gas station and pulled into the lot as the man was saying, "I don't keep up like I used to. I used to know it all—*casus belli, animo belligerandi, animus aggressionis,* all that good stuff."

"I'm going to clean those bugs off my windshield," Roy said, stopping at the edge of the station yard.

"I believe I'll kick the can," the hitchhiker said and crawled out of the car.

Roy stiffened and fiddled with a windshield wiper as the man walked stiff-legged toward the station. It was a quick decision for Roy. He should have known before. But he was caught out.

He hurried around and reached in the passenger window, grabbed the man's bag and jacket and set them on the ground beside the car. Then he jumped in, started it up, and drove quickly away, kicking up a spurt of gravel as he went. *That guy makes me nervous as hell*, he thought.

He liked to drive alone. So what. He had gotten the guy seventy-five miles. That's better than nothing. The Cheez Whiz had made him hungry. He could stop for a hamburger at the drive-through place in Belle Fourche. He could eat it in the park by the river, in the trees out of sight of the road.

VICTROLA-MAN

A BEAUTIFUL girl knelt beside Milk River in the summer of 1930. Beautiful enough that, even though she was simply filling a bucket of water, there were boys watching through the low willows nearby.

It was a large gathering on Milk River just below Harlem, a summer-fair camp that stretched a good way along the south bank, from the river up through the open cottonwoods and onto the broad valley floor. It was only mid-Friday, but the place was filling up fast with wagons and horses and wall tents and a few white tipis. Families were erecting shade arbors at their campsites and thatching them with fresh-cut boughs that smelled strong of the river bottom. People laughed and called and there was the constant sound of stakes being driven. Motorists driving down Milk Valley saw the bright sprawl of the camp a far way off and knew it was a happy one, white and shimmering and wind-pestered like sailboats on a sea.

The girl carried her water bucket back to camp, slowly and cautiously, with her free arm out from her body for balance. Her thin dress snapped in the breeze and her long hair blew

over her face. Her parents were arranging the wood stove in
their shiny wall tent, fitting the smoke pipe up through the
hole in the roof. Her grandmother was patiently carrying
small things from the wagon to the tent. They had arrived
that morning after a three-day trip from the Fort Peck reservation and they had a good place to camp. They had seen
other families along the way bound for the fair, saw them
short-camped on the railroad right-of-way, sleeping under
the wagons, cooking and waving at the passersby. There
were people on Milk River from all over the north—from
Rocky Boy and Crow and North Dakota; from the Blackfeet
reservation and even some tall, stout Bloods down from Canada with their big rawhide drums.

The girl fetched her grandmother a tin cup of water and
then the two of them set about making coffee. The grandmother in the faded calico dress she had washed two hundred times, her head wrapped in a huge kerchief, exhorted
in gruff little notes and the girl responded in her shy
thirteen-year-old whisper. The old woman had all but lost
anything like an appearance—she was worn and erased by
water and wind—while the girl had only recently found
hers, a clear-stamped beauty long known on the continent:
a narrow oval face with a strong wide mouth like a bird and
one dark eye slightly larger than the other, its brow set in a
subtle perpetual arch that suggested both mild surprise and
inborn sophistication with its faint shadow of sadness. The
girl had always spent most of her hours with the grandmother—they were close as sisters—and the old woman
knew well the girl's footstep among many by night. Their coffee was always good, with plenty of sugar.

By late afternoon the drums were sounding from the

dance arbor and the high, driving voices of the singers carried over the camp on the lazy wind. Women hurried to and from the river for water and smoke rose from many cookstoves. It was part of the time and part of the people that everyone cooked the same supper: the salt pork and dried corn soup that was, essentially, *food*, then, up there.

There were specialties available down around the arbor, of course, because it was a fair and people worked hard to find something a little extra during those hard times—things to eat and things to look at. A woman sat on a blanket selling Juneberry soup, and on the other side a woman from Lodgegrass had a kettle of tripe stew she sold by the dipperful.

There was a circular midway around the dance arena. By sunset there were people offering beadwork and featherwork for the grass dance costumes and an old woman selling toys made of chokecherry wood and pairs of buckskin dolls. Soon an old magic man hobbled out of the darkness and spread his blanket on the ground where the firelight from the arbor just reached him. He knew the old-time snake magic and sat there all evening handling his rattlesnakes, passing them over his neck and under his arms and out through his sleeves, with a broad toothless grin on his face. Down the line another magician set up, a big man with sagging breasts and belly and the skipping Alberta accent of the Bloods. A great annual favorite of the fair-goers, he sat heavy as a hill in the flickering firelight, transforming pieces of broom straw into blue-tip matches and changing handfuls of river sand into fine white sugar with a swirl and twitch of his silk kerchief and a few key words. There was a family selling old-time pemmican and an aged man and his boy selling miniature bull boats twelve inches across and painted buckskin tipis three feet tall—things of the last generation, things once living full-scale in the world and now playthings shrunken up small with time-distance.

The fair-goers circled the arbor continuously, dappled with dust and firelight, strolling, watching for friends, and stopping to see the dancers inside the arbor. Until well after midnight the midway was full of the drumming and long shadows and laughter and many dogs underfoot.

Saturday morning the camp awakened leisurely, in fits and starts, with people stirring in and out of the trees along the river, then quieting again. The air was soft and cool and still on the ear after many hours of the drums. The girl and her grandmother had made the big pot of coffee and sat together while the mother was frying bacon. Now and then a car would start or a band of children tear by, off to swim in the river.

Of a sudden the wind rose from over the long narrow camp, and it carried music, a far-off soft song and a light drum. It swelled and ebbed as the wind wavered, but the grandmother caught it like a deer and her eyes grew sharp and at last she stood up from her wooden chair to listen, but right there the wind settled and a wagonload of people clattered by and the song was gone, sank back where it came from.

The old woman returned to her seat. "That was an otter song," she said to the girl. "A very old song. I haven't heard that song since I was a girl. That was one of my favorites." She lowered her head over her coffee cup. The girl watched and reached across to stroke her shoulder through the shiny fringed shawl.

"Nobody sings those real songs anymore," the grandmother muttered. "Nobody knows the words anymore."

The girl stroked the old woman like a cat as they sat quietly. If the grandmother had had the hair, the girl would have
brushed and braided it for her. The wind came up again, and
fell, and rose again, and the people ducked and covered their
faces from the dust, but there was no music on it now. Then
breakfast was ready and the store bread with jelly was passed
around.

Saturday afternoon the crowd began to thicken. Latecom-
ers pulled in on their wagons and unhitched their teams and
local people arrived for a long evening. People were dressed
up a little more for the Saturday night: women in nice plaid
dresses and men with white shirts and their best Stetsons
and neckerchieves. The old ones wore good beaded moccasins and dress-up shawls and full skirts brushing the ground.
There were striped blanket-coats as the day cooled, and
mail-order coats from Chicago. The drums began again and
dust was in the air.

The Assiniboine girl was dressed and ready to tour the
midway with her cousin, an older girl with her hair bobbed
at the ears. They wore their fanciest white dresses and white
stockings and good black shoes. As they left the camp the
girl's mother gave them each twenty-five cents for a treat.

The two girls walked arm in arm around the arbor. The
dust swirled gray-gold in the last sunlight and the girls kept
hankies at their noses. It was a big, noisy crowd that night.
There were gangs of wild young boys careening through and
families walking around together en masse causing traffic
jams when they stopped to visit. There were automobiles

from Havre and Malta with white people in zoot suits and straw hats leaning against them with their hands in their pockets.

It was a surging, jostling crowd and the young girl shrank from it in spite of the holiday excitement. Soon there was a group of boys following the two cousins through the crowd, brash boys with tight white shirts and work boots and flashing eyes. They trailed the girls like dogs and whispered loudly at them and snickered and cringed.

The girls had been around the arbor four times very slowly. The young girl had had enough. It was too loud, too harsh; nothing looked good to her, not the pemmican or even the candy in the big jars. She would come back later when the dancing was going strong and settling people down with watching it.

The girls cut away from the midway, out into the camp, and stopped to get their bearings. As they walked toward their own tents they heard, during a lull in the big drums, a man singing off to their right. It was a quiet, tendriled song and the young girl recognized the voice. It was the man who sang the otter song that morning.

Then they saw him, sitting on a stool before his wall tent, singing, with a kerosene lamp and a woman on the ground beside him. The young girl tugged her cousin's sleeve and whispered in her ear a long moment. They walked softly over to the man and stopped at a proper distance until his song was finished. Then the older girl asked the man if he sang the otter song earlier in the day. The man looked down at his hand drum and nodded, and the girl looked over her shoulder at her younger cousin.

The Assiniboine girl stepped up and shyly asked the man

if he would sing it again for somebody, sometime. The old man said yes, that was what he did at the fair; he was singing the old songs that nobody knew anymore. Sometimes people liked to hear those songs or wanted to hear them to help something turn out right. Sometimes they gave him something to sing for them.

The young girl asked him how much it would cost to hear the otter song and the man shook his head: "Anything you want," he said.

Back at their camp, the young girl brought the grandmother's blanket from the tent and put it over the old woman's shoulders and told her to come on. The woman was up without asking and the two were soon off, huddled together arm in arm.

"I have something for you," the girl whispered, and the woman said, "Oh," and pulled her blanket closer over her shoulders.

They found the old singer's camp and the girl called softly and waited before the tent. They could see old people moving around inside against a lantern's light. Soon the man came out and looked at the two women and grunted. The girl said they wished to hear the otter song and then the old lady said "Oooh" very softly.

There was singing from the arbor, so the old man—he was like a Victrola-man—he motioned them to follow and led the way off behind his tent to a bullberry patch and they stepped behind it and put it between them and the midway.

They stood there, the three of them, in a little triangle. The man was saying a few low preparatory words. A boy appeared with a wooden stool and the old woman sat down on it. Then the man began to sing, just loud enough to hear above the buzzing camp noise and the arbor drums. It was the otter song alright.

The grandmother lowered her head and pulled her blanket up around her neck. The girl felt the little cold bumps along her arms and legs. She knew right then that the song had something important to do with the boy-packs and the river-cool and biting flies in the sun. With her twenty-five cents clutched in one hand, she reached out with the other to take hold of a bullberry branch and she fiddled with it aimlessly while she listened and looked down into the bushes at nothing solid in the world.

SWORN BEFORE CRANES

AT FIRST glance, nothing in the valley appears animate, unless you count the few snowflakes hedging from a glaring white sky as animate, or the ice-edged low-water creeks knifing their crooked ways. Even the frozen dirt roads, snow-white against the pale grasslands, show no tracks or signs of passage.

But when the eye adjusts it sees at last a thin trail of smoke from a wooden house hidden in streamside trees. Then a dark northern hawk shakes itself on a cottonwood limb and from a solitary trailer guyed to a distant knoll a hunched old woman in a black overcoat and calico babushka walks slowly to the hand pump in her yard. That iron and that water will be cold today.

Along the worn highway moves a car from the south. A large, shining American car. Inside it sit two young men absentmindedly listening to the radio. By their cropped hair and antennaless look and skinny black ties, they are Mormons, in search of prey. A man standing by that highway would hear the car coming for a long way, and then hear it going for a long, long way.

At the end of one of the frozen-rut roads, in a home beside a woody trickle of a stream, coffee is boiling for the Keeps Guns. It is a home with all the necessities and arm's reach of a good camp; a smart, durable camp with a multigeneration feel to it.

Two boys are mending a homemade basketball goal near the house. The summer shade-arbor's pinebough roof is sere red and drooping. The outhouse is a patchwork of mixed planks and sheet metal, standing at the edge of the creek's box elders. Near the main house stand an empty eighty-year-old log home, a deer butchering gantry, and a couple of sheds, tipi poles leaning against one of them. Then, the good deep well, engineless cars filled with rough overflow storage, a brown horse and a colt, laundry frozen on the line, a big pile of firewood.

The father of the family is drinking coffee, idly watching the boys hammer down a flap in the backboard. They work with gloves on from the hood of a car. Dogs loiter about the yard. A grandmother sits near the warm stove. A grandchild crawls in the kitchen, rolling an onion along as it goes. The mother sits at the table packing gifts to be mailed to their other boy in prison over in the Falls. She fits in candy and cigarettes and a braid of sweet grass and ties it up good and tight.

It will be Christmas in four or five days and they are meat-less, but they don't dwell on it. They know it but don't dwell on it, because they know in the same way that things will set up in their own good time, or not set up, which is a setup just as well.

◆

ONE night summer before last, up in the Montana Blackfeet country, two boys were driving south on the Choteau highway. They were drinking and getting drunk. The boy driving was a Blackfeet boy, the other was a white boy from Arkansas. They got into an argument over something, probably money, and the white boy reached up and turned on the dome light and pulled out a pistol and shot the Blackfeet boy as he was driving down the road. Shot him dead and grabbed the wheel and pulled off the highway and dumped the body out into the ditch, took his money and cigarettes and Tony Lama boots and drove on. Twenty minutes later a patrol car stopped him for speeding. It was a woman cop. The boy shot her too when she walked up to the car window. At the trial all his family and his girlfriend were up from Arkansas, sitting there stiffly in the stands. They were there to support the boy. They ate at the same hamburger place every night. The girlfriend was arrested for trying to slip the boy a knife in jail.

The same week, down in Miles City, some young Cheyennes were drinking in a bar, getting drunk. These were people who had moved up to Miles to live for a while. They were talking to a white boy, a half-silly boy with a gimpy leg. He was drunk too. They all talked loud and laughed loud and watched on the bias to see if the white boy was laughing as loud as themselves. When the place closed up they all decided to go somewhere together. They got in one of the Cheyennes' car and drove out the Baker road, drinking. The Cheyennes started talking Cheyenne. They stopped at a little park ten miles out of town and stopped laughing and began working the white boy for money. They beat him up bad and stabbed him and he died up under the pines on a pocky concrete picnic table. They caught those kids two days later down in Sheridan, Wyoming.

But the deal that the Keeps Gun boy was in on happened over toward Yankton, South Dakota. It happened a few days after the Miles City incident, in one of those ugly little South Dakota towns conceived when a locomotive stopped for water and a handful of Europeans materialized to sell things to one another.

There was a bully in this little town, a white man about forty years old. He could hardly write his name. For twenty years his family had bullied the Sioux people around this town. Stared at them through slitty eyes. Insulted them so they could hear it. Slurped and slapped at the pretty Sioux girls. Beat up men and spit on their boots, and in winter drove by so they splashed slush on Indians walking along the road.

This one man was the worst of the bunch. Everybody knew about him. The police were afraid to cross him. He was a bully of the sort you heard about in the old Indian stories, old old stories of the half-human bully-monsters who killed people for laughs and took all the good meat for themselves. People used to know what to do in those situations.

The Keeps Gun boy was over visiting people in this town. He was over there for two or three weeks. One afternoon the bully was drinking hard. Then he began driving down through the Indian part of town, yelling at people, insulting them, scaring the children off the streets. The Keeps Gun boy was right there, helping his friend work on his pickup truck.

When the bully drove off, the friend said, "Come on," and they got in a car and drove downtown to the police station and asked them to keep the bully out of the Indian housing before things got bad. Then they went back home.

A policeman pulled the bully over downtown and told him on the qt that an Indian had filed a complaint about him and advised him to go home and sleep it off. And then he told the bully which Indian had come to the station.

Just after dark, the Keeps Gun boy and his friend had the truck running and drove downtown to buy some beer. Keeps Gun sat in the truck while the older boy went across the street into the liquor store. When the Sioux boy was coming out of the store, Keeps Gun heard someone yelling and looked around and saw the bully coming out from a parking lot with another white man.

The bully came at the Indian and grabbed him by the arm and knocked the Old Milwaukee to the ground. Then the other white man tried to hold the boy's arms from behind and in a minute the whole thing blew. Two Sioux boys came running down the street with a hoe handle and they were all swinging and kicking. Keeps Gun jumped out and grabbed a length of two-by-four from the truck bed and ran into the fight.

Some of the other men had clubs as well, but a prosecution expert, and then the jury with tight thin lips, said it was the Keeps Gun boy who caught the bully at the base of the skull with his two-by-four and killed him.

It was nothing like the magical acrobatic antibully finesse of a thousand years earlier in this territory, but the monster was dead and stinking there in the parking-lot lights.

◆

SO NOW they had packed him up some cigarettes and sweet grass and sent it to him in prison over in the Falls. It is two days before Christmas. There will be relatives coming from Antelope and Spring Creek. The grandmother and the mother begin thinking a little more about meat. They haul the big sack of potatoes out from the side room and look them over to see that they are all good. They get out the big boxes of dried corn and check to see if mice have gotten to them and set them out on the kitchen counter. They think about the meat but don't mention it aloud.

Late in the day the two boys are sitting at the table in the house. The women are folding laundry and the father is drinking coffee, looking out at the hills. Then the older boy says, "Let's go," and the two of them get up and put on their coats and retrieve a rifle from the corner and say, "We'll be back later," and leave the house.

They drive in the pickup out to the highway and south a mile, where they turn off to pick up another boy. It is just getting dark. The three drive for half an hour, west on a state highway, then north on a minor paved road, a little-traveled, houseless road that rolls and bucks through the anonymous leased grazing lands toward the rough country of the Cuny Table.

It is full dark now and the work is simple and has been done before. On an open, lightless stretch of the highway they see cattle near the fence. They cut the radio and pull over and check both ways on the road for car lights and put the flashlight on a gaping Hereford and shoot it with the .30-30 from the cab. Two of the boys jump out of the truck and over the fence while the third drives off and up the long climb to the table where he will pull off the highway and wait.

The two boys in the field cut the Hereford's throat and roll her on her back. They set the flashlight on the ground and work with large hardware butcher knives honed on a flat file. They work quickly, watching for cars on the highway. When lights come down the hill from the table, they shut off the flashlight and crouch, ready to run. When the car passes they are back at it. *Wheep, wheep*, a knife whipping on the file. They take just the four legs of the cow, severing the shoulder and hip joints with a hatchet. They drag the quarters over to the fence and under the barbed wire.

They wait low in the dark ditch until the driver comes back down the hill and swerves over to the fence side of the road. They haul the four drumsticks up to the berm and heave them into the truck bed and throw a tarp over them and drive away.

✦

ON CHRISTMAS Day the soup was made and bubbling on the Keeps Gun stove for whoever might want it. It was good old-fashioned soup with dried corn and salt pork and beef in it. There was an inch of day-old snow on the yard where the dogs shivered and wandered from car tire to car tire to sniff the new arrivals: cars and trucks from Spring Creek and Antelope. Magpies sat on the Keeps Gun house watching everything that moved or was about to move.

Inside, the solstitial social heart was beating. The television was on at one end of the room and the radio at the other. The various generations gravitated to their own kind. Children laughed and chased. Three grandmothers sat together in a corner, so old and leaflike and primary that they communicated by the positions of their hands in their quiet laps.

Midafternoon, a Catholic priest stopped by the home with Christmas greetings and a sack of oranges. He was learning to speak Lakota and always told funny stories about his recent linguistic trials and errors. He was a jovial man who wore white sneakers the year round. He sat at the table with mother and father and ate a bowl of the hot soup—*wahanpi, wahanpi,* he practiced as he ate.

The Catholic priest drove off and before long an Episcopal preacher drove in. There was candy for the children. It was remarkably like the Catholic father's visit. The Episcopal was a good-natured man with pink cheeks and pink furry ears. He ate a bowl of the soup and smiled and then the quick receding footsteps—*quack, quack, quack*—on the cold driveway snow just as the day was fading and the dogs were creeping under the porch to their rag beds.

An hour later, the jovial priest was still making his rounds. At the moment he was driving on the dark straightaway past the very pasture where the cow was butchered, driving through the quizzical, caged-bird silence of jovial people alone.

And that night there were those saying that rocks and stones are the oldest things on earth. But there were others who might be saying that that quartered beef lying eyes open in that starry, rumpled Christmas field—that frozen, sleighless, life-biding fuselage—is the oldest thing on earth.

FULL HERON

FIRST, this mild September day—we were afield sketching the big half-yellow White River cottonwoods—there was the red car. We had been following it at a hundred-yard distance for several miles through the Dakota backcountry. Then suddenly on a long empty straightaway its taillights flashed and it swerved to a sharp stop just off the highway. The driver, a Sioux boy, jumped from the car and tore across the road and off into the grassland. Immediately a second boy leaped from the shotgun seat and roared around the car and took off in hot pursuit. They were both sprinting the unmistakable no-joke sprint of the getaway and the chase. Away they went, high adrenaline over the low prairie hills, leaving the car askew with one door open and the dust cloud slowly rising. They were still at it, three hundred yards from the highway, when last we looked back over our shoulders from a rise.

Later in the morning we drew our way down Wounded Knee Creek and then headed slowly into Sharps for coffee. As we passed a remote cluster of homes near the road I glanced over and there, abruptly, near the corner of an aqua

house, was a man of maybe fifty years standing on one leg—
a classic, out-of-the-blue *full heron.*

He wore nothing but plaid boxer-style swimming trunks
(they were no doubt setting up for a sweat lodge) and was
standing—free-standing—idly in the warm sun while
younger men moved here and there about the yard. His left
foot rested just above his right knee; his right hand was
cocked on the right hip and the left hand lay naturally on the
hiked left thigh. Utterly relaxed, easy as a leaf in that ves-
tigial stance, he seemed to rise from an alternate, other-
postured world.

I remember an old photo of a native Australian standing
that way, leaning on his spear. And I remember faintly a thin
boy from grade school days who stood like that for long ses-
sions on the grass beside the village swimming pool, with his
skinny arms wrapped—several times it seemed—about his
neck and upper shoulders, his chlorine-riled eyes blinking.
But that was thirty-five years ago; and this was a full-grown
late-20th-century man.

It was only noon and it had already been a full-blown September outing, heavy on the buckshee. The green and maize
crayons were worn to nubs and flocks of piñon jays cried
above the pine hills. And the two microcurious, sky-lit sight-
ings—ha, I thought, a double yolk of a day. And that made
me think of the Blackduck brothers.

Wilson and William Blackduck, twins, up in the Tongue
River country. I knew them obliquely, ten years ago. Observed them, more than knew them, but we had some good
talks on occasion.

They were men in their seventh decade, nearly identical

twins of great beauty and refinement. Six-foot full bloods of slender build with small braids from fine heads of hair, the braids joined across the chest at clavicle level by a single strand of colored yarn. They too had a memorable way of standing, an exemplary, brotherly way, at a certain gentle, well-calculated angle to one another. Large silk scarves knotted at the throat and roomy old sport jackets and good felt Stetsons. They were so handsome and reflective and fine-minded that for them to simply be there in front of the grocery in town or at a community gathering, standing there gracefully and even-footed with Stetsons in hand, gazing quietly off, was enough; an accepted duty, a benevolence, and enough.

They had grown up during the hardest of reservation times, stood through famine and Caucasian glower and toxic bureaucracy, and swam daily in the Tongue. As a young man, one of them (I forget which) had "done things." He discovered at sixteen that he had certain gifts and one time he used them to good effect: When a cousin was involved in a legal scrape, the Blackduck boy sat down alone on the night before the hearing and concentrated hard on the matter. Next day at the courthouse a key piece of evidence had vanished from the file.

The brothers went to the army, together, for the second war and were prisoners in a Japanese camp for most of a year, together. They were held at a supply depot where all day long they carried boxes of sundry explosives for transshipping, while the Japanese guards laughed and prodded and cautioned them not to stumble and fall. Evenings, the guards would sidle in to smoke and ask them why the Indians even bothered to fight for the white Americans, a question the Blackduck brothers pondered, briefly, looking at the ground.

After the war, back on Tongue River, they resumed their even lives. They ran a few cattle and ponies and raised children and weighed their people's ways and smoothed them best they could for the second half of the roaring century. By the time I knew them and watched them they had been standing some thirty years since the war, reassuring, sensible, calm as horses.

Then William died, late one summer. Wilson sat alone all night and by morning had decided what to do. He walked to town and told the old man running the trading post that he wanted to sell the family bundle, then walked back home.

The trader made a phone call and that afternoon two men in suits drove into Wilson's yard. The two strangers were excited, but they acted cool as cucumbers and loitered an extra minute beside their car, jingling the change in their pockets, mock-yawning and stretching and mock-watching the magpies jumping in the pines.

The Blackduck medicine bundle had been in the family for three generations. It was well kept and even famous. A hawk-skin headdress, an ochred crane wing, a miniature lariat and hobble, a rawhide silhouette of a stallion, various paints and herbal specialties and spherical stones, all in a rouged rawhide pouch worn smooth as driftwood. Wilson got a good price for it from the strangers, enough for the two ample family grave plots he wanted and for a good gray headstone with Blackduck in small clean capital letters. He even had enough left over for a quick trip to Oklahoma in the fall.

I made a small pencil drawing of Wilson one day, with his

hat in his hand. I saw him several times before he died. He was virtually alone by then, with a deaf and sickly wife and his children gone to Billings. He occasionally mentioned the sale of his bundle. He considered it a desperate but heroically timely deed and spoke of it with relief and fatalistic gratitude, gazing out the window with that look that was enough all by itself.

One day as we sat there he chuckled and stirred and said, "But I still have some things like that, too." And he reached under the bed to pull out an eighteen-inch wooden box and placed it on his knees. Chuckling, he opened it and showed me his new arsenal against ill fortune: an array of Catholic-saint medals; a rabbit's foot on a chain; a plastic shamrock; a peyote button in a glass box; a J.F.K. dollar; a buffalo tooth; a splintered four-inch piece of palm leaf from a Palm Sunday service; a venerable turkey wishbone. . . .

◆

THE Blackduck brothers. The little drawing of Wilson, I realize each time I see it, is sadly incomplete and single-yolked: Wilson alone, standing in that memorable way. I have been often tempted to take it down from the wall and open it up and add the other figure, work him in there at that delicate, mirror-image angle, but it would be working from sketchy, one-legged memory, and so far I haven't had the nerve.

Silent Herder

SUMMER evenings when the light softens and the air sets, you will see boys materialize from various points of the little village and walk heavily to the playground of the knoll-top school. Two, three, four of an evening, they straggle in and take, each, privately, to one of the playground swings with a discreet distance between them and slowly begin to swing. They are lovesick Arapaho boys, sixteen and eighteen years old, and their swinging as the night falls is pensive and stop-gap. Their long black hair flows and buckles with their arcs. They gaze off at the tail end of sunflare behind the Wind River mountains or at the dusky river course, August-salty, to the east, below. They will swing in rhythmic silence through the sunset and well into the dark before they wander off in various directions and finally home.

Tonight a dog trots from behind the school building and crosses the thin gravel of the schoolyard, casts a quick accustomed eye at the faint *chee* of the swing sets. It is the black-and-white panda-faced bitch from the east edge of town going home after a day of foraging. Behind her trots her longtime friend, a brown guppy-jawed powwow dog with thinning hair and prominent sunburnt teats like a Berkshire sow. They had been out along the Little Wind River and up one of its feeder creeks and back past a rural soda pop store where they whiffed at scattered candy wrappers and watched a spry old whippet–Saint Bernard cross pull over big trash drums and rustle through the contents on the ground. Now, with her usual timing, the panda dog would get home just as the lights in the family house come on and the supper scraps are cool on the counter.

◆

TWELVE miles away in a roughhouse motel in the lee of the foothills, a young man was dressing and watching the darkness come on. On the desk a feeble lamplight fell on the remains of a quick meal: wads of hamburger foil and a cottage cheese carton and a bag of green onion potato chips.

The man was dressing and his girlfriend sat curled on the bed simple as a rabbit, watching him while the haywire television flickered and bucked in the corner. Her blond hair was up in curlers. The man was skinny and strong and bore a birthmark the size of a fifty-cent piece on his right rear shoulder, a brownish green birthmark frilled around the edges like a lichen. He pulled on a long-sleeved black workshirt out at the elbows and spattered with red paint.

"You be there—that's the main thing."

"I'll be there."

"Just be there, no matter what. Either way I'll get there, so you just sit tight and wait."

"I'll be there," said the girl.

The man tied a dark blue bandana around his head and put on black canvas running shoes and tied them good and tight.

He wore a commando sheath knife on his belt and hung a short lanyard around his neck with a tiny black flashlight on the end. He flashed the light twice to check it and finger-brushed his little yellow mustache in the mirror. Then he picked up a small haversack, looked into it a moment, and said he was ready.

They drove through the dark ranch country and onto the reservation. They knew where to go and what to do, best as they could figure; they had given it a flyby that morning. The girl drove to the little town where the lovesick boys were still swinging and dropped her man at one shadowy corner where a dirt road cut off from the highway. The man said, "Just be there." He quietly closed the door and slipped into the dusty elms along the ditch.

He followed a brushy row of poplars across a long vacant lot, past a rambling dark brick mission building. He stopped every few minutes to catch his breath and listen. He skirted a squat, boarded-up riverstone building and followed the edge of its brushy yard until it abutted on the big open sundance grounds. A single arc light burned from its pole on the school knoll off to his left. Around the edges of the half-mile-square sundance grounds scattered houselights twinkled.

He rested there a moment in the ratty lilac hedge at the school boundary, then set off, walking quickly, across the dark open field. In a few minutes he could make out the sun lodge in the center of the grounds, its cottonwood pole structure and the bright offering cloths tied to its high rafters. A minute later he was inside it, kneeling behind a log strut to rest and listen through the dense dark.

He breathed hard with excitement and looked up at the tall center pole of the lodge, straining to see what was up there at the top. Eagle feathers, he hoped, lots of them, tied there among the religious offerings at the sundance ten days ago—prime tail feathers he could turn in Denver or Albuquerque for twenty-five dollars apiece. He tightened his pack and swiped his mustache and crept over to the center pole. He looked up along it and nudged it a little and made ready to shinny up.

He was up there, hanging like a monkey high on the cottonwood pole, twisting and leaning, trying to see around him, with his arms and legs aching and burning with the scrape and strain, when the panda bitch at her home just east of the grounds knocked a water bucket off the steps and the man inside walked over to his screen door and looked out and saw a quick flash of light from the sundance lodge. He knew immediately what it meant—any of the three thousand Arapahos would have known—and hurried across the room to call the tribal police.

The man on the sun pole sensed it a few minutes later, then saw the cars hurrying out from town. *Screw.* He slid down the pole and dropped to the ground and beat it out from the lodge and across the field. Just in case, he pulled out the feathers he had cut and threw them aside as he ran. He dodged brush piles and the debris of old campsites and hopped the fence into a pasture and away. Looking back as he ran he could see the police had cut their headlights and were trying to come in on the qt, but he was way ahead of them.

He found the girl right where she was supposed to be, waiting in the pitch, and they scrammed back to the motel. The man opened a beer and washed his scratched-up forearms. Then he began to worry and fidget and after half an hour they threw their things into the trunk and drove up into the mountains and slept in the car. They were safe, they figured—nobody had seen a thing, not the man or the girl or the car. The owner of the panda-faced dog had wiped out the stew pot with a crust of bread and tossed it out the door to the dog after the excitement was over.

The couple drove away before daylight, headed north. Two hours later they cut east and climbed into the Big Horns where they paused at the edge of a fragrant meadow to stretch and the girl set her slightly blurred eye-catching beauty in the sun for a minute before the day grew hot.

Then they dropped down the mountains and curled into Sheridan where the man had a cousin. They found the little house on a tattered edge of town and the three of them sat in the backyard all afternoon drinking beer. They talked about going up to Cavalier County, North Dakota, to see an uncle and maybe find a week or two of late summer work. It would be something to do. The cousin strolled casually over to urinate behind a shed. He wasn't wearing anything but blue jeans. As he walked back toward the chairs he paused at a three-foot cedar and lifted his leg to it dog-style, grinning at the man and the girl.

They slept late the next day and left Sheridan at midafternoon. They had a small bag of groceries and a pint of peppermint schnapps. They drove north into Montana and struck the Yellowstone valley and followed it northeast in the last of the lingering daylight. The two men smoked Wolf Brothers crooks and listened to the thin night radio while the girl dozed on a pile of bedding in the back seat.

The cousin shifted and pulled one bootless foot up and under him and broke a long silence, grinning suddenly over at the man behind the wheel.

"Remember when we used to drive over to Ten Sleep every Sunday and watch the Girl Scout busses unload for the camp?"

The driver glanced at him sharply and threw a quick flashlight of a look into the back seat.

"Cheap thrills of youth," the cousin said, looking again out the dark window.

Somewhere north of Glendive that night the man spotted a lonesome grain elevator standing by railroad tracks and pulled off the highway, in behind the building. He spread a blanket bed across the front seat. The girl slept on in the back and the cousin made a bedroll under the rear of the car on the cheesy old blacktop of the granary lot.

❖

THE girl awoke at a distant sound. Then again: *pank*. It was just daylight, the first leak of sun showed on the high white elevator walls. She rolled and dozed again. *Pank*. Now she knew what it was—the pellet gun—and even, in a split second, where she was. Her man was awake, slung low in the front seat, shooting pigeons from the window when they settled around the elevator to feed on runaway grain.

Pank—and a flurry of flapping wings. Then the girl dozed, drifted gratefully into the headless and footless horizontal world. She was warm and happy. She had a brief dream with her hometown in it—O Walla Walla—a snatch of fearless willowware dream with people sashaying in the street.

Pank. She opened her eyes and heard the cousin stir under the car. She had forgotten all about him. She knew they had donuts in the rear-window bay and would soon find gas station coffee. Later they would stop to broil pigeon breasts on the rusty hibachi in the trunk. They would have them on bread with bright yellow mustard and a cut-rate dented can of hominy. She was happy. She had been happy for six months, but this was the happiest she had ever been, so far.

F. O. B. FLICKER

A BOY walked through town, cutting along the swayback dirt alleys. Some days he took the alleys to avoid the townspeople on the streets; sometimes he took the streets to avoid the snarling backyard dogs in the alley—a half-breed boy. Either way, it was the end of July and the town was full of dusty hollyhocks and late afternoon pools of shade and young flickers cried all day from their nest holes.

He walked along until he saw the circus poster on a telephone pole. He had forgotten all about that. He read the poster, then cut three blocks over to where the circus was just setting up on a vacant lot at the edge of town.

It was a small outfit for sure—half a dozen stubby house trailers and two large trucks with Texas and Florida license plates. The boy walked shyly around the doings. The people he saw looked foreign and distant. Even though busy at their work they seemed angry and unhappy. A lone man smoking a cigarette behind the big animal truck glanced at the boy when he turned the corner, but never acknowledged him— just looked off over his head.

The boy walked completely around the edge of the camp

and then sat down on a slope fifty yards away. He watched a circus woman staking out a pony and a fancy horse. A baby elephant stood near a truck, eating from a pan on the ground. The best thing he saw was three men driving the stakes for the large tent, the way they got their sledges going in rapid-fire order on the same stake—*clink-clink-clink, clink-clink-clink*—as fast as they could go.

Next morning the boy walked back to the circus grounds and sat on the same slope. By now the big tent was up and people were moving about getting things ready for the mid-day performance. The woman was saddling the fancy horse. She got on and warmed up the horse for its dance routine: sideways, backwards, round and round in a rocking, pretty-boy canter. None of the circus people seemed excited; they had done all this 500 times across Nebraska, and Kansas, all the way from Texas. A juggler was strolling around tossing colored balls in the air.

Then the boy saw Crow coming across the field. He watched him coming across, his long braids bouncing, and knew his friend had seen him sitting there. Hé. Hé.

"You going to the circus?"

"No."

"You doing anything now?"

"No."

"Come on then. I want to show you something."

"Show me what?"

"Something you've never seen before."

They walked off. Crow's step was quicker than usual, the boy noticed that. They walked three blocks and cut in through the bushy backyard of an old house. Crow led the way, in through the back door and across the yellow kitchen.

In the next room, Crow's cousin, Hill, was sitting at a cluttered table. There were lots of beer cans. Hill was just sitting there bleary-eyed and smoking. He looked up at the boys. Hé.

On the mattress against a wall, a large blond woman was lying, asleep. She was naked. A corner of bedsheet hid her loins. The rest of her body was uncovered, in the sprawl of deepest sleep. After a moment, there was the smell of wine rising from her deep, slow breath.

Crow whispered to the boy. "She works at the circus."

Hill looked over at them. "Florida." He smoked and his gaze fell back to the ashtray.

The boy looked at the unconscious woman—her large splay breasts, the mottled pink and white thighs, the shaved armpits. He took a short step toward her, out of politeness to Crow, and looked again at the breasts and the full belly, then stepped back by the table.

Another boy came quietly in the door with a friend. They sidled into the room, glancing quickly at Crow and at Hill, then gaped at the sleeping woman. Hill looked at them after a while, then got up heavily. He walked quietly over to the woman and crouched by her feet. He reached out a finger and gently tickled the sole of one foot. The woman hardly stirred, but on some convoluted reflex cue her loins pumped halfheartedly three or four times, far removed, ventriloquial, ghostly.

No one said a word. Hill sat down heavily without a look. Crow and the boy sat across from him and made baloney sandwiches on the cluttered table and ate them. Now and then another schoolboy would materialize and tiptoe into the room and peek at the mattress.

Then there were four old men, wrinkled and thin. They arrived in a group—the boys heard the four car doors slam softly out front—and walked in very slowly, very formally and respectfully.

They removed their Stetsons and walked in a silent line past the mattress. In the dull gloaming light of the room, it was like a line of well-wishers filing reverently by a casket. And that is what the boy remembered for many long years: the eerie decorum, the slight shuffle of feet and clothing and a trace of guarded, proprietous public breathing above the heavy, oblivious, shore-like breaths of the girl.

EUREKA

WE WERE taking the ranch folks into town for Saturday night dinner at the old hotel. The five of us gathered at the loose-jawed gate in the fence separating the house and its big cottonwoods, the hired man's trailer, and the bunkhouse—the domestic ground—from the wide open range.

We got in the rancher's car and eased across a cattle guard in the just-dark onto the two-rut ranch road. One of the dogs slinked out of the headlights trailing three feet of duck entrails—they had found the place in the hay meadow where we cleaned the birds that afternoon.

It was a slow six miles down the sandhill valley to the state highway. All of us had been outside a good part of the October day at our various pastimes and we were all similarly tired and hungry and vaguely happy in the towering American emptiness.

The car's headlights bounced and cast above the elemental road, illuminating the soapweed, an occasional jackrabbit. Earl drove carefully at ten miles an hour, working the changeable road, swerving to avoid soft spots and high centers. The car swayed steadily and restfully and brought forth easy, restful talk of past work and like seasons.

At one point in the fence line the rancher told us about a heifer on the adjoining spread that he sometimes saw near here, a long-legged white Chianina heifer that looked more like a horse than a cow. She was a jumper. Earl saw her take the fence one day effortlessly, from a dead stand, right along in here. His wife had seen her too one evening. We all talked about that for a while, just before we got to the highway. She was the embodiment of the simple extraordinary the long blue day had stirred us to expect.

Then we climbed up onto the paved highway and zoomed south for the remaining twenty miles into town and the talk changed. We were rushing now; the talk was more brittle. Earl told us about his two favorite greyhounds—fast brindle dogs—finding a bucket of coyote poison mixed with antifreeze in the barn last winter. They died tangled up together on the trailer stoop.

We all had steaks at the old hotel, big rawboned steaks sprawling over entire plates. We ate quickly. The horseradish went round and round, and then we left with our toothpicks tilting and zoomed off on the highway over the hills.

When we passed the entrance to a big ranch in one of the broad lake valleys—there were two pickups there with their running lights on, talking head to tail, like horses in flytime—Earl jerked a thumb that way and told me a story about the late owner, a tough, land-rich woman who had lived several miles back in under mansard roofs and walked among the first and only topiary in the sandhills. She died a few years ago of sour-mash whiskey.

She was widowed early and lived most of the time on a big

spread just south of the Badlands, up in South Dakota. She was managing just fine, kept all the ranches going. Then one day her teenage son didn't come home from school. This was 1957. Everyone looked for that boy. They had sheriffs and detectives and airplanes and bloodhounds, but they couldn't find a trace of him.

After almost a year she was done in. Then someone told her, why don't you ask some of the Indians, see if they might help you. The woman drove over to Rosebud and found a medicine man there and asked him if he could do her any good finding the boy, dead or alive. That old man was afraid to try it, they say—you must be careful about finding lost persons, because sometimes the things in charge will demand another person to replace the found one. It is a delicate, Archimedean operation. He turned her down, but told her about another man over on Pine Ridge, over around Kyle.

So a few days later she drove over to Kyle and asked around for George Thunder and finally found him living on Medicine Root Creek some ten miles out of town.

This old man was a very traditional man. He knew all the old ways. He dressed in the old way, wore a cowboy hat and neckerchief and a six-shooter in a holster. A proud man with the look and loft of one whose grandfather had frozen to death in 1910 and whose distaff grandmother had starved to death along this very creek in the winter of 1921. A traditional man with ancient manners who clasped your hand each time you met: If you encountered him on the street a quarter hour after shaking hands with him outside the post office, you would shake again—a single, soft shake—and feel the better for it.

This man sat down and listened to the story and the stack of things behind it, and the timbre and tone of the woman's voice and the magpie chatter down by the creek, and finally agreed to try and help the woman find her boy. Dead or alive. He looked at the ground and told her, come down here next week. Bring along a couple of your good horses, and I will try to find out something.

So she did.

Meanwhile, word spread that George was going to put on a *yuwipi* to try and help the woman. Groups of relatives began straggling into his place and setting up camp near his little cabin. Soon there were several white wall tents standing and half a dozen old cars, with good wood smoke coming up from the stoves in the tents and people eating and visiting around. This might be something to see if George could find that boy through his medicine powers.

And then, on the right day, the woman and one of her brothers and some of their family drove in two spanking pickups with a horse trailer behind, with all kinds of food and presents for George and his kin. The woman stopped her pickup and asked this and that question of this and that person and finally knew where to park and they all got out of the trucks and waited.

As evening came on a ragged circle of people formed at a discreet distance around the lodge where George would conduct his *yuwipi* ceremony. George had been taking the sweat baths all week, getting ready. Now he came over to the woman and shook hands and looked for a long time at the two horses she had tied beside her trailer. Then he pointed at the big black one and said, tie that horse outside the *yuwipi* lodge.

Then, when it was full dark, he began. The woman and her family sat in chairs thirty yards from the lodge. The woman was chewing lots of Blackjack gum. The horse was tethered right in close by the lodge. When the songs started suddenly within, the horse jumped a little and strained on its rope, but not for long.

The woman watched, chewing her gum with a stop and start rhythm. After the first singing there was low talk from within the pitch-dark lodge, then more singing and drumming. Then George's helper lit a kerosene lantern and began to tie him: fingers and hands bound together with sinew strips; feet and legs together. Then he wrapped him in a big blanket and tied the blanket tight around his neck with a hide rope and wrapped him all the way down to his feet with the blanket and the rope. He was bundled up like a cocoon.

The helper lay him down carefully, blew out the lantern, and then the singers began again, loud and high. Now they were calling in the spirits from the night to help George find out about the boy. There were many songs and the sound of gourd rattles and muffled voices. The black horse stood at attention, ears up. The woman sat in her lawn chair and stared hard at the dark lodge and the nighthawks swooped by.

Two hours later the singing stopped and the lantern was lit and there was George, sitting calm and disheveled beside the folded blanket with all the sinew cords and the hide rope coiled neatly on top. It was all finished and soon the women came out from the wall tents with kettles of food and everyone ate.

Finally George sat with the woman and her brother and after a while told them what to do. They should drive back to her ranch, get up before daybreak and, just at dawn, they should turn the black horse loose. George would drive over to the ranch later in the morning. At high noon they would start out and trail the horse and see what developed. See what the horse had learned from the *yuwipi*.

The Thunder party arrived at the ranch at eleven the next morning, ate at her table. At noon they got in their pickup with one of the woman's nephews and started off on the black horse's trail.

They followed that horse thirty miles due north, up past Kadoka. Then the tracks cut west for a few miles and eventually dropped into some rough country with a stream running through it. When the party drove up to the lip overlooking those breaks, they stopped and got out. Down below they saw the black horse grazing near a grove of trees.

George and the others watched the horse silently for a moment. Then George turned to the nephew and said, "I think you better go and call the sheriff now."

George never took a dime for doing that *yuwipi*. The woman moved down here to this ranch a short time after. They found the boy's body right down in that grove where the horse was grazing.

Earl shifted to a higher pitched, end-of-cycle chronicler's tone older than Sennacherib: "That was nineteen hundred and fifty-eight."

Then, at a landmark it would take weeks to master, he slowed and found the gate and crept back onto the sand road and into the slow sway and we all changed our positions slightly for the terrain and its roll. Autumn grasses rustled and swiped at the underside of the car. We were quiet and sleepy by now; our toothpicks hung idle in our hands.

I was thinking lazy thoughts about the "Black Houdini" I had seen once on the sidewalk of New Orleans, an affable Jamaican man who "escaped" from a strapped-up cardboard refrigerator box eight or ten times a day for the tourists' coins—when there she was at the edge of the lights, the white heifer: cool and collected, she stared big-eyed for a split second, then she was up, birdlike, owllike, over the fence and gone.

A Rainy Tuesday

I CAME over to ask you about something—

We were a wealthy family a long time ago, up there on Bow River. A family with horses. My father ran a famous herd up there, all good paint horses. It was known all over that country. People used to see it from the Canadian Pacific trains going through. People talked about those horses.

Then it all went bang. Everything went bang. This was sixty years ago in the Bow River country west of Calgary. My father and his brother went on a big hunting trip up in the mountains. They rode up through the foothills and they just moved that horse herd along with them. They hunted a long time over there—two or three weeks—and then they started back. They came over the Simpson summit with a whole lot of game packed up and all those paint horses, moving along nice and slow and enjoying themselves.

Then a big storm came down. Lots of snow. All the trails were closed up. Things were bad. They managed to break a trail with the unloaded horses and followed behind with the pack horses and the wagon. They crossed Bow River up in the foothills and got the herd up onto the Canadian Pacific right-of-way. The snow wasn't so deep up there and they started making better time.

Then that freight train comes along. They heard it coming and then they saw it. They tried to get those horses off the tracks but they wouldn't get back down into that deep snow. They just milled and jammed up and carried on.

That train never even slowed down. Ran right through them. Most all of the herd was killed right there. The men managed to get their wagon and team off out of the way. So they had that. But it was a total loss for them.

My father was in a daze for a long time after that. Everything gone, just like that. His brother was broken in two by that day. He was broken by the strain of that business and died not too long afterwards.

My father walked around in a daze. He tried his best to get back on his feet. Tried to make some good money from hunting and trapping, money to start over with. He had an old jalopy to get around in. But by those days that country around there was hunted out. There wasn't much fur left.

A couple of years he tried that, working hard, but never could get ahead. He never got over that day with the train. He knew he wasn't a cattle-raising man—didn't go for them. So one day he got the family in the car and drove away.

We drove over through Medicine Hat and over through Assiniboia and stayed there a few days. Then we came down into the states, down around Wolf Point, Montana. There are some Assiniboines living down around there. We stayed there all that first winter, stayed with some relatives north of Frazer. We helped them cut wood every week.

There were some wealthy people around there in those days, too. People with lots of horses. There was a man there with a real big herd, pretty near three thousand head. That winter about Christmastime his boy got sick. Bad sick. Everybody had about given up on him.

The father heard about a medicine doctor way up in Canada. Old-time medicine man. They said he could cure anything. The father of that boy sent for that Cree doctor and he came down to Wolf Point right away. And, Hé, sure enough, he cured that boy.

The father was so happy he gave the doctor five hundred horses, and the doctor went back to Canada. How he got all those horses up there I never knew. After that, in the spring, the father put on a big giveaway for his friends and neighbors around Wolf Point. To show his thanks for his son being alive.

It was the biggest deal they ever saw up there. He had a hundred good buggies brought in on the train from Minneapolis. And dozens of wagon wheels. Gave them to everybody. Things people could use and enjoy. He gave away some more horses, too.

I think all that kind of made my father sad. It made him think about everything lost. So that summer he got everybody in the car again and we took off. Went over to Fort Belknap for a while, then down to the Crow reservation. I remember that trip. We took our time. That summer seemed to be a good year for sage. The hills up in Montana were all kind of blue with it, kind of turquoise with it on the hillsides. We didn't have much extra money so we would stop every day along the road and pick chokecherries and buffalo berries and eat those all day long, with bread.

We stayed there around Lodgegrass with the Crows. My father and my older brother hired out for farm work around there. We stayed for the winter. My mother had some friends down there.

Next summer my father decided to take off again. We left just after the Fourth of July. Drove south into the state of Wyoming. I remember that trip, too. It was hot. You saw the meadowlarks hiding down in the fence-post shadows it was so hot. My father watched the sky for rain clouds coming in over the mountains and tried to get under them to get some rain. Pulled off and waited and hoped that cloud would come over and rain on us.

We went around the Big Horn mountains and stopped at Wind River reservation for a rest. Went right up into the Wind River mountains to cool off. Right there on Wind River is the only time I ever ate sheep. Not bighorn sheep; regular sheep.

We were coming down out of the mountains one day, feeling good. We started to get hungry. We were so poor we didn't know what we would eat. Then my cousin saw some sheep off in a little valley. They were all crowded inside a big old section of eight-foot culvert pipe that was laying there just over the fence, kind of smashed up. Those sheep were in there out of the sun.

My cousin never even thought about it—he just stopped the car a ways down the road and jumped that fence and crept back on that culvert. He snuck up from one side, you see, so the sheep wouldn't spot him. He got right up there and half-nelsoned one of the sheep when they broke out of the pipe. That's the only time I ever ate sheep in my life.

End of that summer we took off for Oklahoma. We made gas money picking up chains and other things we found on the road and selling them for scrap. We got to Oklahoma and stayed there two years. We had some relatives down there in the Kiowa country. At first we would do anything for money. One time the whole bunch of us had a job to trim grass around some tourist cabins beside the Carnegie highway. All we had was our hands, no tools. There we were, six of us on our hands and knees pulling off that tall grass by hand. We did it right too, every inch of it. When we got done it looked like somebody had gone over it with a mowing machine.

Later my father got some regular farm work with a German family. We stayed there two years, then we headed back north. We had a better car then, too. A Pontiac—that's a good Indian car. Came up through Nebraska and worked for a week in the potato diggings down there. Then came on up here to Flicker River. I've been here ever since. My parents are buried here. My father got himself one pretty horse before he died and he used to stand there a long time looking at it.

But we always made it all right. That's why I'm glad to be here. I've seen things and places and I'm happy to be here, living.

And now my son-in-law has some trouble, and I need a ride up to Sharps if you're going up there today. Someone came along last night and poisoned his horses. He had four nice bay horses in a field along the road there. Someone came along in the middle of the night and gave them poison feed. Three of them dead so far.

So I wanted to go up there. I wanted to ask you for a ride up there.

The Nomad Flute

THE FAN belt broke at so gifted a place it would have been heartless to complain. The ash trees in the coulee heads were pulsing golden and when I pushed my car off onto the shoulder and climbed to a knoll near the fence line, I could see the processional bottomland trees of the Missouri River not so far ahead. I hoped there would be a phone there at the crossing because I hadn't passed a ranch house for many miles to the south.

I locked up and began to walk the dirt road toward the river. It was a bright end-of-October afternoon and the slight steady descent to the great Missouri was a pleasure in itself—better to walk it than drive it, after all. In half an hour I had topped the last of the river-edge hills and looked down on the Missouri itself, low water but eminently respectable as she eased through the sagebrush flats.

Below, where the road struck her, I saw a ferry outfit, and beyond, on the far shore, a ranch house and buildings where the ferry keepers no doubt lived. A thrifty little spread with cattle grazing on the uplands and turkeys creeping through the river brush. Ferry operators would have to have a tele-phone, I thought as I started down the hill.

The ferry was a simple board-bottomed flatbed with a good-sized outboard engine built into it, the whole thing buttoned to a thick cable stretched across the flow between two pole-and-concrete bastions. The craft was just lowering its snout to meet the gravel bank and set down a large Jeep full of hunters and a pinto setter. When they were on their way I spoke to the helmsman and he said to come on over to the house and I could call up to Havre.

We ferried across in a cloud of engine fume, a ride of maybe one full minute. The ferry tender was a tall ruddy man, quiet and easy; when he lifted his Stetson to wipe his brow I saw the sharp line across his forehead where the sun-red broke off. The interior of the house was well-cool and still and, one felt immediately, under sure choreographic control. The woman of the house was there, waiting. She too was tall, but far from ruddy. Large and handsome, she struck me as someone I had seen in some semipublic place, and I thought of a photo on an album of piano music or a book jacket—she had that sort of carriage and posable poise.

They were both calm and cordial. I placed a call to Havre for the auto-parts store and soon learned I couldn't get the proper fan belt until, most likely, Monday; it had to come in from Great Falls and then be driven down to the ferry. The couple seemed pleased to offer their accommodations for the weekend. They stood there shoulder to shoulder, smiling. This was Friday afternoon. There was no real alternative, so I resigned myself to a close view of the upper Missouri for a couple of days.

The man called out the back door and soon a boy of ten

strolled in, a dusty serious lad with a straw cowboy hat in hand and a red sun-line of his own across his brow. He shook hands with me and took me outside and across the road to a long three-part garage where he cranked up an old Chevy pickup. He sat on a tattered chair cushion in order to see over the dash. His father ferried us across and we drove back to my car. The boy was amiable, but oddly businesslike. He exuded preoccupation with some important, perplexing problem that kept him scowling mildly at the skyline even while we made small conversation.

We towed my little Japanese station wagon slowly back to the landing and parked it off to one side. The boy looked over the car as though he were studying a stud horse for soft spots, and he seemed to find it a bit weak through the withers. I grabbed my suitcase and a pair of good books and carried them over to the house, made two phone calls and went back to my bedroom. I had spent the preceding two nights in the back of my car and was ready for an hour's nap.

When I rejoined my hosts there was, I thought, a bustle in the air that was almost festive, that didn't feel quite every-day for the tone and drape of the house and its many basking violets. The woman was busy in the kitchen but she took a moment to show me the large wandering house. It was all very simple and down-to-earth, but directed in a delicate way that was admirable and cozy. She then sent me off with the boy to see his arrowhead collection. His room seemed sober and bare for a young lad. A neat row of boots and shoes along one wall; a .22 rifle leaning in a corner; a red-leather Bible on the bedstand. With the trace of knit in his brow, he showed me a pair of rusty muleshoes he found at a nineteenth-century trail-ford up the river.

I stepped out into the yard to smoke and check out the setup of the ranch. The north-south road—the only real road crossing the river for forty miles in either direction—ran between the house and most of the ranch buildings. On the far side of it I saw a large barn and then a smaller one with a pair of sheds at its side and then the long garage. To the left of the barns in a small fenced-off area stood a cottagelike dwelling with its windows open and pale curtains blowing in the breeze.

On the near side of the road behind the house lay a sizable garden and several beds of cutting flowers hamstrung and singed by a recent frost. On the north side stood another white shed and the entrance to a fruit cellar and great piles of friendly ranch junk waiting on call. At the far end of the truck patch was a chicken coop and then fruit trees in staggered rows that stood out sharply against the dense rusty-green of the cedar shelterbelt where turkeys trotted after late grasshoppers in the ragged grass. It all fit neatly into the narrow valley. Above the shed roof the low, worn river bluffs rose quickly and took their place against a blue fall sky.

We sat down to dinner at six o'clock—the hosts, the boy with his hair wet and combed, and myself, when suddenly a young woman I hadn't seen before joined us. There was a salver of fried ham and roast potatoes and baked yellow onions and applesauce and a dish of last-of-the-garden. The woman told me they used to have a good many guests at the house; they actually boarded an occasional hunter or party of canoeists descending the river. So they were used to newcomers at table and rather missed the visitors. She had her black hair pinned up with a barrette in it. She talked well, floating a bright, three-dimensional conversation. Her husband was quiet corroborator, smiling and nodding. The boy looked off at whatnot while he chewed. The young woman was silent. She must have been twenty-five, cast in a thick, insular morph that radiated both isolate vigor and mysterious inner doings.

The ranchwoman filled me in on things in general. They had a married daughter in Missoula and a younger one in private school in Missouri, in addition to the boy—he broke his revery briefly to send me a twitch of a grin. We soon discovered that we shared a common origin, the woman and I, back in Ohio, and in a few moments had narrowed it down to a startling degree. She had been raised in a town of 15,000 just half an hour from my native village. Within the stroke of three sentences we were each poised with our forks halfway to our mouths—she knew my hometown rather well, had had a good friend there and had visited frequently. I knew the family of her friend in a general way, knew their house, not far from my parents. There was a moment of simple disbelief and childlike suspicion before accepting the coincidence and releasing the frank glint of mutual wonder and connection in the eyes. The husband chortled and the boy looked up.

The woman had left Ohio in 1949, moved to Wyoming shortly after high school to stay with relatives. There she had met and married—the man nods slowly, yes, by Johnny, he was there. They then came to the upper Missouri country in Montana and ranched not far from their present home. They took over the ferry operation (it was one of a handful of state-subsidized ferries in the bridgeless remote of the outback) when the husband injured his back. They still ran a few white-faced cattle along the river. They sometimes chafed at being tied down by the ferry from April to October, but on the other hand, as the woman put it, it was "more social than pure ranching."

We talked for two hours after dinner. Now we had connection, and when I lay in bed that night I found myself thinking of the quiet residential block in my hometown that the woman knew so well forty years ago. I conjured it as I dozed off, the very block of small white houses with titmice in their trees. . . .

❧

THE next morning after breakfast I walked out and down to the ferry landing. Traffic was heavier than usual, they said, with the bird hunters coming and going to and from the public lands, loads of men from Billings or Denver with dog cages and cases of dark rum in their campers. One group got out of their truck to pose for a photo on the ferry barge before heading south.

I wandered back away from the river toward the barns. I glimpsed the strange girl going into the garage, but when I passed the open bay doors she had disappeared. I walked around the small barn and the cattle lot behind it and then passed the little cottage bunkhouse. There was an old man sitting in the yard oiling his work boots and I stopped to say hello, eventually sidling in through the weak wire gate to his yard. His name was Harold Soldier and he worked for the ranch doing anything that needed doing. He was familiar with the western Montana town I lived in, had been there once or twice for basketball tournaments when local teams made the grade. We smoked and chatted and watched squadrons of ducks fly up and down the river. There was a small garden patch browning in a corner of his yard and when I left he invited me to take one of the pale softball-size watermelons lying there—"But if it kills you, don't blame me."

At lunch—the woman made me a tiny, photogenic tuna sandwich—my hosts told me about Harold. They had known him for more than thirty years. He was a Gros Ventre man from up around Hays and could fix about anything broken on earth. He was in the army at the tail end of World War II and a year or so after it was all over he brought back a wife to Montana: a Belgian brunette whom everyone said was a gypsy. The ranchwoman remembered her but hadn't known her long. Harold and his pretty gypsy wife settled into their new life working at a far-flung ranch way up on Cow Creek. The girl didn't quite know what to make of it, but once curtains were up and Harold rigged a phonograph for her to play her Django Reinhardt records she made it OK for a while. Her accent soon became famous around the territory and all the Indian veterans of the European theater made a point to stop and say hello and talk of places in the war. She worked hard at everything, cooked and washed and ran a stringy flock of chickens. Carried endless water and fought the 'hoppers, but the Django bop eventually thinned on the wind and it was just too much for her. She disappeared one day after three years. Nobody could figure it out—she was clear of eye and strong of teeth and she seemed to care a great deal for Harold.

And Harold Soldier, poor man, was completely baffled. He felt no malice whatsoever and what pain there was came forth as a strenuous effort to comprehend and explain this almost preternatural severance. During half a year he would shake his head slowly, looking at the dry earth, and ponder it and tell the ranchwoman how much his wife wanted to speak French again; she missed it badly and often chattered in it to herself, and Harold proffered the theory, born of some late cloud-mooned night, that she had run off to Canada for that very and noble purpose.

A few years later Harold moved down here and went to work full time. "He'll be here tomorrow for Sunday dinner," the woman said. "He eats with us every Sunday. He's welcome all the time, but that's the way he wants it."

That evening the ranch couple and I sat down for a drink before dinner. The woman was spruced up in a nice dress, strong and calm and quite beautiful. After a while she said, "I can show you something from back home," and left the room to fetch a dulcimer and set it on the low table before her. It was a crusty old thing that had been in her family a good while, she told me, having been carried over the mountains to Ohio from eastern Pennsylvania. She teased it a little and finally broke into a halting pretty tune that clanged and bonged about the halls and crannies of the house. The husband smiled good-naturedly at the odd sound in his ear. The music was anachronistic and lovely in the late afternoon stillness. When she finished I said I could almost smell the honeysuckle and I think she knew what I meant.

The strange girl was back for dinner, suddenly there standing behind her chair. She was spruced up a bit too and the puzzling time-lag sensation was stronger than ever. Her hair was plaited and coiled on her head. Her eyes were a serious midsummer blue beneath dark thick brows. Her nose was slightly upturned, with frank functional nostrils. The cheekbones were high and slavic and she bore faint, downy, Idaho-shaped muttonchops to her jaw. She stood, gazing away, with a composed vacancy. Her other-century look was accentuated by an odd assemblage of clothing of timeless cut and grade: neat, clean, but somehow out of kilter, "Albanian," and then seamed stockings and blocky heavy-heeled patent shoes. She responded when spoken to during the meal, but the dense magnetic field was never broken.

I retired to my room early and lay down to read with my window up. "A German Idyll" by H. E. Bates. Later, just before sleep, I heard a party blow their horn for the ferry and minutes later the muffled clank and bustle of the engine as it crossed to pick them up.

Sunday morning the boy was assigned to drive me out to see old tipi rings on the bluffs three miles upstream. We took his pickup as usual. He had opened enough in my presence by now to sniff a rudimentary laugh when I made a joke or crossed my eyes at him during meals. He maneuvered the truck along a rough track and finally pulled up at a level knoll and parked amid a dozen tipi rings of pale stones like fairy-ring mushrooms melting in the grass. It commanded a fine view of the valley and we spooked two whitetails from the brush below.

Later I took another smoking stroll around the ranch grounds, thinking to walk up the road a ways. As I passed the small barn I saw the girl duck into its doors with her arms full of something and I decided to follow. I was curious to speak with her alone, to see what she was like on her own. I turned into the barn within a single minute after she had entered, but she was nowhere to be seen. It was obvious after a glance around the place that she had seen me coming and had either fled or was hiding, perhaps watching from a mow, so I walked out and on across the yard.

Old Harold was in his chair again so I stopped for a chat. I sat on his steps while we listened to his portable radio bringing in weekend football scores from across the nation. Harold annotated an occasional town or region when it struck him: The Bluffton score reminded him of a Mennonite conference he attended there long ago and the Kansas score he associated with a great niece who studied nursing there. And in Philadelphia he once spent a few carefully inlaid days unwinding from boot camp. At one point the boy drove by and gave us a businesslike nod. Harold said, "That fellow ought to go to a picture show."

Eventually we walked over to the house together for Sunday dinner. They ate that meal in midafternoon, the way I like it. The strange girl was absent and I took the opportunity to ask about her, casually, but the woman simply said, "She needed a place to live." The woman wore a slim peach dress for the Sabbath and again there was that pedigreed something in her pointed aplomb and her tossed-back head. Harold and I demolished the better part of a huge beef and turnip pie and a deep plum cobbler.

The lady was feeding waxwings, a flock of Bohemians that showed up on a quick north wind a week ago, and after dinner and our separate ways I slipped into my room and poured a jigger of whiskey from my flask and sat alone in front of the bay window for half an hour watching the beautiful birds feeding on raisins in the yard. One group would flutter down from the tree to feed for a moment on the ground, to be replaced, gently, by another in a near constant flurry both gregarious and civilized. They were located on

the west side of the house and caught the five o'clock sun—
svelte, immaculate birds down from Jasper or Lake Louise,
dropping from the trees soft as ash, gorgeously detailed and
perfectly painted, all the fine points radiantly and lovingly
there. . . .

Late that night I was awakened by a faint door slamming
and had a silly inadvertent vision of the boy in plaid pajamas
slipping along the hall and into the strange girl's room, and
then the sleep-hazy conclusion: "So that's what they've got
on their minds."

The next morning everyone was busy with Monday business. I gathered my things and by half-past ten the service-
station man was there with my fan belt. I said good-bye to
Harold—he was meticulously coiling friendly old scrap
wire—and walked to the ferry to say good-bye to the man.
I offered him money for my board. He refused a cent, but
then said, in an afterthought way as I turned, that he could
use an old-time number seven iron bean kettle if ever I ran
across one.

I found the woman in the west yard broadcasting raisins
for the birds and we had a warm good-bye that brought the
humble coincidental glint back to our eyes. I said I would
stop again when out that way and I drove slowly off through
the grounds thinking how much better it all was than a simple bridge over the river. The girl with Albanian muttonchops was elsewhere as usual. The boy was backing a tractor
out of its bay as I passed and he responded to my honk with
a matter-of-fact index-finger salute and a quick spit over the
rear tire.

❧

THE following spring I travelled east for Easter with my family. It was a cool bright Sunday wet around the ears and the village maples were vivid with red blossoms showing like mulberries against bare branches and leafless blue sky.

There were relatives about, the small house was ajostle with several persons too many, squeezing by one another in the short hallway and taking turns at the loo. For the midday meal we had a ten-pound fresh ham grazed with garlic and basted with stale beer. When we all gathered around the long drop-leaf table my father bowed his head abruptly and set his face, closed-eyed, for the paschal grace.

"Dear Father in heaven, we thank you for the blessings of this day and for the promise of this season. We thank you for health and good food upon our table. For family and loved ones to share this holy time. Help us to make the most of our opportunities and to appreciate the beauties of this life and grant us the strength to do thy will. We ask it in Jesus' name. Amen."

Then he rose and put the "Russian Easter Overture" on the record player and set to carving the chestnut-colored pork. Throughout dinner he clowned for the cousinage and razzed his younger brother with shadowy references to chasing country girls through summer dusks sixty years before. Every quarter hour, as the wine went round, he broke into a bar or two of "Roaming in the Gloaming" and grinned mischievously at my uncle, who shook his head with a blank helpless look and the entire table tittered and stirred.

After the meal a few of us adjourned to the side yard to take in the afternoon. My mother and I ended up alone in the wooden swing sipping California brandy. From the small yard partially enclosed by young elms and catalpa trees with

wild grapevines hanging from them, we overlooked the back
lawn with its fierce new green and its kitchen garden half-
spaded where robins hopped, and beyond, the dull red-
brick buildings of the village square. Jonquils were on the
verge of blooming and a single yellow tulip raised its head.

We talked a little, but mostly we listened to the new April
goings-on, the various robins caroling about the neighborhood and titmice whistling high in the trees. I could hear
three cardinals (a bird I never heard in the West) in full song,
calling from three different directions and planes. I placed
them instinctively in trees of yards I knew from long ago: the
far one, two blocks off, beside the house the Groves girls
lived in twenty-five years back; another over by the one-time
Ronda Rathburn home on Vine Street; and the third straight
south, in the maples showing their uppers just above the
community library.

The latter treetops struck me, when I looked off that way,
hit me with it all again: they stood along the muddy block
the woman at the ferry had spoken of, and I told my mother
again how strange the meeting had been, how casually it sur-
faced and gelled.

"She is a beautiful woman," I said.

"She always was a beautiful girl," Mother said. "I remember her. I met her at the Harvey's once or twice. She came
from a very good family."

After a moment of shooing away an early insect, she
picked it up again. "She left in kind of a hurry," she said,
giving me a look I knew well, a quick, dramatized scowl-
grimace with an eye roll worked in, conveying deep com-
miseration with just a trace of censure.

My eyebrows rose spontaneously. Just then my father

called from the window above us announcing that he was about to play his timeworn "Crepitation Contest" record for the cousinage and inviting us inside.

"I think we'll pass this year," I said, and when our proper silence was restored my mother filled me in in a low, slow voice.

"It wasn't too long after the war." The girl was a banker's daughter over in Martin. She had just begun college at a hoity school nearby. She was going strong with a prominent Methodist preacher's son. One October night—I was already picking up a strong imago of 1949: smoky autumn light on the mothball fleets, Miles Davis doing "Godchild"—one October night her parents and his parents and some of their tuxedoed friends came home from a social outing and found her with the boyfriend in his car, parked in the driveway with the motor running. Carbon monoxide had got them. They hadn't a stitch on when they pulled them out. The girl was unconscious. The boy turned out to be dead.

One of my cousins came striding around the corner of the house, still grinning from Round One of the crepitation contest. He wore a jaunty yellow boutonniere and carried the brandy bottle mock-hidden inside his suit coat. He always had the finest timing in the family. We laughed and held out our glasses saying, "Yes, I do believe I will."

Near Michaelmas

Two men stand in a village park one hot September. They stand quietly, tall and slender, side by side with their heads down and hands clasped behind their rumps, in the cool spray of a lawn sprinkler. Flocks of shiny grackles feed methodically on the light green manicured grass nearby.

A police car has slowly circled the park and now pulls up near the men. Two officers climb out and amble across the lawn. When the wet men see the policemen coming they step softly out from the hose spray and into the shade of a hackberry tree.

"Good afternoon, gentlemen," one of the officers says. The two wet men grunt politely, nodding.

"We're looking for a dog," the other cop says. "An Irish setter. A red dog. Have you boys seen anything like that?"

The two men shake their heads quickly.

"OK," says the cop. "The way it is, the owner of the dog saw a man with a red shirt on fooling around with her dog just before it came up missing. We noticed you're wearing a red shirt. That's all." He nods toward one of the men.

"Yes," says the man. No more.

"Do you boys live around here?" asks the officer.

"Yes," they both answer. Then one says softly, "Red Shirt." The other says, "Lost Dog."

The policeman nods and glances at his cohort. The two wet men are obviously stone sober; their English is a little weak, that's all.

"OK," says the cop. "This woman who owns the animal, she thought maybe someone walked off with her pet. . . . So you haven't seen a red setter dog running around then?"

One of the wet men looks up, points at his friend and says, "Lost Dog."

The officer chuckles and glances at his cohort again.

The cohort speaks up. "Where have you boys been this morning?"

One wet man says, "We just came into town this morning."

"From the reservation?"

One man says, very softly and politely, "Red Shirt." The other, "Lost Dog."

Both cops grin, lift their caps and run their fingers through their hair. One of them steps back and gazes at the red-shirted wet man.

"Well, I guess there's likely to be six or eight fellows walking around in a red shirt on a Saturday morning."

The wet man in a plaid shirt yanks his thumb at his own chest and says quietly: "Red Shirt."

The cops laugh.

The wet man in the red shirt touches his hand to his own belly: "Lost Dog."

The cops laugh again. They think the game is getting good, whatever it is. Then the wet men laugh a little, getting

into the spirit of the thing, looking back and forth quickly
from cop to cop.

One of the wet men, still laughing lightly, asks the policeman for a cigarette. The officer pulls out his pack and gives
the two men smokes and lights them with his lighter. As he
puts his cigarettes back in his uniform pocket he asks, as if
he had almost forgotten, "Where are you boys planning to
spend the night?"

The two men nod together, saying at once: "Red Shirt/
Lost Dog."

The policemen stand and look at them. Finally one of the
cops slaps his hands together, turning and glancing about the
park. "Well, screw it—let's go scout around a little more."
They say good-bye to the two men and walk back to the patrol car.

They felt good, friendly, relaxed. Cosmopolitan even.
Their verbal assets had been subtly frozen; autumn seemed
imminent even through the strong late heat.

THE END OF
JOHN SADDLE

JOHN Saddle had been having bad luck for a while now. It began when he was booted from the town of Flicker. For years since the Second World War there was a tent and shanty Indian camp on the north edge of Flicker. It stood in a broad grassy field just beyond the stockyards. Lots of people came down from South Dakota to shop in the Flicker stores, and when they came in those days they usually set up tents and stayed to enjoy themselves for a time. There were fifteen or twenty tents that liked it there well enough they became permanent citizens. John Saddle was one of these. He lived four years down there and nearly called it home.

Then one summer the community leaders of Flicker decided the tent town was getting out of hand. It was a bit larger each spring, they noticed, and there were more and more idle shantytowners killing long sultry days on the street corners. So one afternoon a group of businessmen collected a dozen moribund cars donated by the Flicker auto dealers and drove them out to the tent camp and told the people they could have the cars for their own if they packed up and drove them straight north to South Dakota and didn't return. All but one of those worn-out cars made it back to the reservation and even ran for a week or two thereafter. The one that guttered out on the Slim Butte road was John Saddle's; he had to unpack his belongings and pile them on top of the old Chevy just behind. And so he lost his Flicker home and his new vehicle in one midsummer swoop.

Back in South Dakota John moved into an empty cabin in the hamlet known as Number 9. Local jokesters called it Sioux City. It was a decent muddy little village out of the way of things, with deer heads tossed on the roofs to weather away. John lived there a full year and made it OK, but his luck, to his mind, never got any better. He sat there in Number 9, eating light but never complaining, and then one day he died, rolled off the old kitchen chair in front of his cabin, where a neighbor girl saw him and ran for help.

They carried John Saddle down the dirt street to the community hall and into a small back room and laid him out on a cafeteria table. In a few minutes the village medic arrived and soon the neighborhood priest. They looked John over and listened to his chest and then straightened up and pronounced him dead. The medic went off to call a physician to certify the event and the priest conscripted two Christian women from Number 9 and sent them to bathe the corpse and prepare it for eventual burial. The women undressed John and put his clothing in a plastic bag and covered him with a U.S. government sheet.

They gathered their towels and basins and returned to the little room with a bucket of hot water. They were speculating whether the water was too hot to be used on a corpse and wondering if it mattered at all, when they opened the door—and, lo, there sat John on the edge of the table with a sleepy look on his face, idly scratching his lower back. The women hollered and one scurried for the priest, and soon people from the community hall offices were coming back to peek in the half-open door. The priest trotted in and whispered with John, asked him a question or two he couldn't answer, and insisted he sit still with the sheet and a green army blanket around him.

In half an hour the doctor drove in from a nearby town. He listened, scowling thoughtfully with his chin in one hand, to the story of John's revivification and examined him thoroughly, then pronounced him fit and functioning normally. The people in the hallway looked at each other wide-eyed. The doctor and the priest conferred briefly in a far corner. John put his clothes on and thanked everyone in the room. He stopped by the coffee-maker in the front office and drank a quick black cup, then walked slowly outside and down the street to his cabin, with everyone in Number 9 watching secretly from their windows.

John stayed inside for two days, sleeping and gathering strength, before he walked back into town and down the street to check his mail at the post office. It didn't take long for him to see that things had changed since his unorthodox solo flight. People avoided him in the town, crossed the street hurriedly to escape his path. He felt the sudden irrational sour of the social-caustic that first hour out and knew that his pole star had changed, and all the world with it.

John was viewed by his townmates with a virulent form of the suspicion provincials hold for widely traveled neighbors. He was, since his one-hour ellipsis, considered foreign, spooked, and even touched. Always a minimally social man, as his image curdled in the eyes of Number 9, there was no net to hold him. Months passed and John's outcast life fell into a lazy neglect. He conversed with no one, hardly even the postmistress when he stopped there. He began to frequent the garbage cans behind the community hall in search of scraps. He became the shepherd of stray dogs; half a year after his false death he had eight mongrels living with him and every new moon seemed to bring another. His one social occasion was a visit to an old man he had known all his life. Once a month John walked four miles to his friend's rural home and the two of them would adjourn to a sagging engineless Oldsmobile parked off behind the house. There they could sit in peace, away from the grandchildren, and talk a bit for half an hour.

It wasn't much of a life, John knew, but it meandered on, off-key but steady, for two years, and he had almost come to accept it as normal, when one summer day the sheriff and a deputy drove up and announced that there was a rabies scare in the county and John would have to give up his dogs. They herded them, all sixteen of them, into a paddy wagon and drove them off somewhere to shoot them in a gully. The whole episode reminded John again of his rotgut luck.

Now, without his fawning watchful dogs, John cared for nothing much. He decided to give up his cabin in Number 9 and move into a half-shack on a hill across the creek, where he would be less bothered by his fortune and its social stigma. He put up his old wall tent from the shantytown days and lugged his few possessions up there and put his kitchen chair in the shadow of the tent. There were a few scraggly wild plum trees at the edge of the hill and a blanched tailing

of household trash from previous tenants trickled down toward the creek. There were a hundred small marrowbones
and a thousand bottle caps trampled into the dirt of the yard.

John sat there all alone every day with the look of a calm
shipwrecked man. All because he had dived and resurfaced.
He didn't even visit his old friend anymore. The village
dwellers could see his tent up there on the hill. There was
one old lady who dropped off a sack of potatoes now and
then. When cold weather came, John moved into the half-
shack and stuffed the cracks and soon had a low-profile rust-
colored mutt sleeping under his table. There was an abandoned country church half a mile downstream from his camp
and he walked down there twice a week to pull boards off for
firewood. By spring all four walls were stripped naked to the
studs for seven feet above the ground and John figured he
had come out even.

On a warm April day when John was loafing in his kitchen
chair watching the plum blossoms on the hillside trees, a
shiny car pulled off the road and drove back toward his tent.
It was John's half sister from Rapid City and his nephew from
California. They were driving around visiting relatives on
the reservation. The man hadn't been home in nine years.
The two got out of the car and stood a little uneasily after
saying hello. They looked on and off at John in his chair and
the stained wall tent whiffling in the breeze and the cedars
on the hills beyond.

Now John hadn't spoken for four or five days, but he had
something he wanted to talk about, and this was an unex-
pected opportunity. He cleared his throat and with his eyes
on a marrowbone told his guests that he had finally had some
luck. Just last week he had gone over to check his mail as

usual and the postmistress handed him a large envelope from some sort of Grand American Sweepstakes. The envelope looked almost like a telegram or newspaper headline and it had his name printed in big letters and said right there in plain English that John Saddle of Number 9 was a big winner in the thing—maybe even a millionaire, or at least a cabin cruiser or a fancy car.

"I hope I get the money," John said. "I'd rather have the money. The letter said four to six weeks. I'm going to build a nice big house right here on the hill with plenty of room for anyone who wants to come and visit, and always have good things to eat."

Late that afternoon John walked into town to check his mail; he was keeping a closer eye on it now. Returning home he found a single English walnut lying beside the road. It must have hopped out of someone's grocery bag. John picked it up and took it home with him in his shirt pocket.

Back at his table, John ate a slice of bread with Karo syrup on it. Then he fished out the walnut and looked it over and shined it on his sleeve. He cracked it carefully with his hand axe and spread out the meats and picked through them happily, chewing them up slowly fragment by fragment. He lay down to bed that evening still dislodging an occasional morsel of nut from his teeth and chewing it up with appreciative little bites. And then, shortly after midnight with the plum blossoms dancing, he died again, and stayed there this time.

TOTEM

ROY turned east onto Route 20 and leaned back to get comfortable. It was good to be on paved road again. He was off
and running for three or four days and that made him happy.

He laughed again thinking of Dick that morning. Roy had
seen him shortly after leaving home; as he approached Dick's
ranch lane he noticed him walking out toward the road with
a rifle. Roy pulled up near the mailbox.

When Dick got near enough Roy yelled. "Whadya do, find
a big snake?"

Dick said, "Naw," and kept coming until he leaned in the
passenger window of Roy's car.

"Naw. I tell you: There's a dead steer lying over there that's
swellin' up and stinking so bad I can't even sit in the yard
after supper. It's right upwind. I figured she'd be blowin'
pretty soon, but she hasn't. Thought I'd come down and put
a hole in it and get it done with."

They talked for a few minutes and Roy drove off. Several
times that morning he thought of Dick out there shooting at
the bloated carcass from a discreet distance. He thought of
it again now, accelerating onto the highway, and wished he'd
brought a six-pack of beer with him. It was getting hot.

The hotter it grew the flatter life in Wyoming settled;
spread and flattened and sank. The Rattlesnake range shim-
mered off to the south—uranium country, baking and fum-
ing. Only the big hawks had an option and sailed high up to
tilt and drift. Everything else curled up, flattened, and
closed its eyes like a man trying to hide and sleep at the same
time.

Roy drove through Hiland, where a pathetic pontoon
rusted steadily in the weeds, and tiny Waltman, hiding and
sleeping, and then he saw the handful of buildings ahead
that comprised the hamlet of Powder River. Roy always
slowed when he saw that place ahead, set himself in a certain
way each time he passed through the town, once or twice a
year. There was a thing there that set him off, jelled him. He
never really anticipated it, but he knew it when he got there
and welcomed it as an atmospheric change, like a small gust
on a heavy day.

It was a simple enough thing that set him off: a remnant
sign of a defunct roadhouse that hung from a tall pole above
a rotting parking lot. It read: Romeo and Juliet Cafe. It
wasn't any sort of casual speculative whimsy that stirred
him. He knew the rectangular concrete-block place from
thirty years ago when he was in high school and lived forty
miles to the north and west. The high school kids used to
stop there for hamburgers on major outings.

The Romeo and Juliet wasn't named by an itinerant Shake-
spearian or even by a jerkwater wag. Romeo was a man of
Basque descent; his father had ridden a train in to the edge
of the Bighorns for a sheepherding job. Juliet was a large-
hammed Wyoming woman.

The particular scene Roy thought of as he passed through

the village was senior prom night, 1954. Three couples, including Roy and his date, met at the Romeo and Juliet after the dance. They drank beer, screwdrivers from a bottle, and sloe gin as they drove to the place. They ate hamburgers at the counter and talked loudly in their suits and formals in the bright inner light. Then they decided to go out along the Powder River to a place they knew, to drink a little more before going home.

Out there, at a long abandoned farmsite, they stood around the cars in the warm May night listening to car radios and getting mildly drunk. To this day, when Roy heard the word *love* in a song he associated it vaguely with a feeling of buoyancy like the one he felt that night on the upper Powder River in his charcoal-gray church suit with a red carnation and his big black Florsheim shoes.

He remembered that night as strongly as any scene in his life. Of course the annual driveby reinforced it regularly, kept it green. Other than that, he remembered very little from his past because it was not given to him to do so. A few faces, a fishing trip or two. If one pushed him he would eventually recall the day a pair of turkey vultures vomited on him in his uncle's Indiana woods when Roy blundered beneath their nest tree.

But the prom night was his primary pole star, the single reading from which he continuously receded. The six kids drank in the '54 moonlight. They walked about the old homesite with their screwdriver bottles in hand, exploring the sheds and the bank of lilacs.

Roy and his girl were holding hands and strolling along a rickety windrow of cedars and elms, when they came to a concrete shell sunk into the earth; an old root cellar perhaps, four or five feet deep, the concrete shining silver in the moonlight.

They walked dreamily along the edge of the pit. Roy was just beginning to think of things romantic when his date glanced down into the corner below and jumped back with a start—"Skunk!" she cried.

Now this was the part of the story that set Roy off and made him squirm in his seat and glance uneasily around the horizon every time. He had been a bit drunk that night, he knew that, but it must have been more than that. He had been lifted by a vodka-washed chivalry; he had astonished himself.

Tossing his screwdriver bottle softly to the ground, Roy vaulted into the cellar without a thought and attacked the cornered skunk with his big black Florsheims. He kicked the animal when it tried to scurry by him, knocking it back into the corner. The skunk released its spray, but it was too late. Roy was on it with his big hard-heeled shoes; a quick one-two stomp to the head and the animal shuddered and lay still. It had taken fifteen seconds.

Roy, now that the stench had hit him, the gagging bio-syrup caught in his throat, jumped out from the hole, cursing, and ran back toward the cars. His date was there, relating the story. They were swearing and guffawing in disbelief. Roy's suit was so saturated with skunk oil he had to take it off and throw it into the lilacs and put on an old mechanics overalls from his buddy's trunk. His girl drove the car home while he sat in the back seat, stunned.

That little chivalrous moment would become a minor legend in the area. Roy never knew that, but the tale was kept afloat by a recitation every few years by, perhaps, a rancher off to the east or a car salesman out to dinner up in Greybull. Roy would return in a couple of days to see about the suit. He would certainly retrieve the big Florsheims. He and the prom girl would remain friends, but nothing ever came of it.

Stupid, he thought now as he rolled east from Powder River. *Stupid*. He raised himself up from the seat enough to loosen the trousers from his groin.

The stink of the skunk brought back the stink of the turkey vultures in his uncle's woods. A skunk and a buzzard, he thought. What a team. It was the first time he had associated the two images, the first time he held them up together, one in each hand. It made for a burning, salty continuity he never knew he had. It was stupid unto greatness. He reached for a stick of beef jerky in his glove box. He would stop for a six-pack first chance down the line, at the Natrona store.

The Committee

IT WAS a good day for a committee meeting. Two days' wind had blown the wet out of the roads. The meeting was held at George Swallow's place and there was an imposing gumbo hole midway on the half-mile lane, but today it was all right if you knew where to hit it.

The Swallow house was new, sat in a fenced-off yard with a weak garden in one corner. Just beyond the rear fence the land jerked up and climbed toward the piney ridge. On the front walk slept a short-haired honey-colored dog, a female whose teats were still swollen and red from a litter; she had been sired by a transient hunter's weimaraner and whelped on the edge of Bullhead by a calm yellow bitch from the Wakpala region who had followed the scent of a church barbecue thirty miles and stayed.

The committee men began arriving about ten in the morning. Eddy pulled in in his '75 Monarch and the dog got up and moved off of the sidewalk. The other men came in a new Chevy Blazer, a powder-blue Ford pickup, and a red Skylark. With each arrival the dog got up and moved a few unhurried steps farther from the walk.

They were all there except Henry. They drank coffee and shot the breeze in the living room. George's wife was hanging wash in the backyard, trying to keep things from stripping off the line in the wind. Finally Henry drove up in his two-tone station wagon and went inside. The men greeted him and one said they were afraid he sank and drowned in that big mud puddle on the lane, and Henry said he knew enough to wear a life jacket when he came to see George. The committee was in session.

George Swallow poured another round of coffee and picked up some papers from the kitchen counter.

"OK. We're going out to see about some things this morning. We're going to look at the new community building and see how they're coming along on that. They're supposed to have that done by middle September.

"Then we're going to stop by Joe All Night's place and talk to him about that trailer. He's got to move that trailer off that old tobacco-garden site. We had the old folks go down there to make sure—he's right on that thing, right where the tobacco garden used to be. That's a sacred spot. We've got to talk to him about moving that trailer fifty yards up or down. There's lots of room in there. We've got to get down there before he gets a well in.

"Then we're going to discuss this visitor problem—all those people coming out here this summer to go Indian. We've got a busload coming in from New Jersey and a big bunch from Germany. We've got to discuss that situation."

The men finished their coffee and retrieved their Stetsons and left the house. Three of them got in the Blazer and three in the station wagon. They drove five miles north on the highway and turned into a muddy construction drive. They looked like a committee the way they drove, slow and looking-all-around. They got out of the cars and gathered on a knoll overlooking the building site. All six men wore blue jeans and plaid shirts and good pointy boots. They stood up there for a few moments looking over the basement excavation, the crew of big red cement trucks, and the construction company trailers on the far side.

George Swallow and Eddy walked down the hill to talk to the foreman and make sure that the main meeting room was going in plumb east-west the way the tribal council wanted it. The other committee men waited on the hill, smoking and looking at the sky. Pretty soon George and Eddy returned and said everything looked pretty good. Some water in the hole for sure, but pretty much going along on time.

The committee climbed into the cars and drove off, north again, and then west on the Rabbit Creek Road. Henry was wondering how Joe All Night would take the news about his trailer.

George said, "He'll take it all right. He hasn't got a well down yet. If he had a well down it would be different."

The Blazer turned through a gate into a handsome half-moon bottom and drove slowly back to a white trailer sitting near the stream. A dark green Oldsmobile was parked there, showing the ravages of heavy hail. A long-boned, panda-faced dog born on a feed sack in a trashy patch of sagebrush near Dupree came around the corner and grinned at the committee with a slow-wagging hairless tail.

Then Joe All Night and one of his kids came out of the trailer and greeted the committee. The committee men stood and leaned against the Blazer and they all made easy small talk for a while and looked up and down the valley and at the hills across the creek.

Then George said he came to talk to Joe about the old tobacco-garden place and told him how the old people had been down here last week and pointed out the place where the Rees had their sacred tobacco patch a long time ago and it turns out Joe's trailer was right in the middle of it. The tribe wanted to keep that spot as a special place; fence it off out of respect for the Rees and all the Indian ancestors.

George took Joe over a ways from the other men and showed him the boundaries about where the garden used to be. They stood over there by themselves, pointing and kicking thoughtfully at the grass as they talked. Then George and Joe came back over and all the men said good-bye and the committee drove away.

George said, "I told him we'd get a lot of men out there to help him."

The committee drove back to George Swallow's place and went inside and sat where they sat earlier that day. George poured more coffee and the men quieted.

"OK. Now we're going to talk about the visitor problem. Now we got some letters from people who want to come out here this summer and go Indian for a few days. We've got a bunch from New Jersey coming out and a bunch from Germany. OK—now I think we're going to have a schedule problem here. Looks like they're coming on the same weekend."

"What are they after this time?" one of the men asked.

"They want to camp someplace and have some ceremonies and go up on a hill to fast. See if they can get a vision."

"Ah—hey, those Germans better be careful, they might

get a vision of Adolf Hitler and start something. Ha! How many of those Germans are coming out?"

"About fourteen."

"Don't tell old Ernie about that. He saw enough of those Germans in the war. He'll get his uniform out of mothballs and get after them—ha!"

"Hey—you write to them and tell them to bring plenty of good beer along."

"OK—now we've got to figure out where to put these people. Someplace they can camp and go sit on a hill. Now last year we put people over around Pretty Butte. But we can't put all these people out there."

"We've got to be careful about fires with those people, too. They might be greenhorns."

"We'll keep an eye on them."

"Get the Dog Soldiers to patrol around there. Keep an eye on the fires."

"Keep them from chasing our girls around."

"OK. We'll put the Dog Soldiers on security."

"Those Germans want their own sun dance, too?"

"Ha. Maybe next year they'll want the sun dance."

Eddy looked out the window and saw a tired corkscrew-tailed dog with matted hair come limping across a field toward the house; one of its forebears had slinked tail-tucked into a chokecherry draw and hidden there during the Slim Buttes fight in September 1876.

"OK. We can give one group Pretty Butte. Now where can we put the other bunch to keep them out of trouble?"

"How about that old rodeo grounds over at Snake Butte?"

"Ha. OK. Is that water pump still working over there?"

"Last I knew it was working."

"Maybe we'll go ahead and let the Germans have Snake Butte. They can climb up there and have all the visions they can get. OK. We'll put the New Jersey people at Pretty Butte and the Germans over at Snake Butte."

"And get the Dog Soldiers to keep an eye on them."

"We'll get some Fox Society men to help out if we need to."

"How long are they going to camp over there?"

"Four, five days. July 15, 16, 17, 18."

"Maybe we can get them to do a rain dance for us."

"I don't care what they do as long as they don't burn the reservation down and they stay away from our girls."

"And don't bring any U-boats!"

"Ha. OK. No U-boats on Indian lands. We'll put up a resolution on that."

"OK. That's that. I'll get Thelma to write up the letters." George picked up his sheaf of papers. "OK. We got the building site checked out. Joe's going to move his trailer, and we're going to give the Germans Snake Butte."

Chairs scraped and the committee men rose and set their cups on the table. "Next meeting in two weeks. At Henry's place." The honey-colored dog heard them coming and woke herself from a sleepy dream to move off the sidewalk as they came down the steps.

PAGING CHARLES
LOWBOY

THE woman in the messenger-red coat had crossed the highway and given them the news. In the half hour since, the tall old man with the salami nose had been dressing: climbing slowly into his black suit pants and clean white shirt, rigging his cuff links and shining his long narrow shoes with a corner of the bedspread.

Elmer, a very old man who lived in the cabins across the highway, had died that morning just before daylight. Charles Lowboy was dressing to go to the family and sit with them in neighborly condolence for the afternoon and probably on into the night.

Now he stood beside his wife, bending to enable her to reach his necktie from her wheelchair. His vision was too far gone for the fine work. Hazel tugged at the wide tie and straightened the big knot and slapped at a speck of lint on his suit coat.

"Now don't forget," she told Charles, "Elmer's brother is related to some of those Big Legs. He married one of those girls from Hisle. Those Big Legs were connected with my mother's people a long time ago. My aunt married one of those boys. They lived over by Allen. You tell Elmer's brother when you see him; he'll know. That's Donald. Not Donald Junior, Donald Senior, from Hot Springs. You tell him who you are."

She turned Charles around to inspect his backside and then pulled him over her and straightened his thinning hair with a crooked arthritic hand. Her voice was strident with excitement but her touch was soft, had butchered many deer.

It seemed they went through this procedure every two weeks anymore. The woman knew the connections and the bloodlines and the circumstances-in-the-wings. Charles was the ambassador who attended the wakes and spoke for their family in his handsome dark suit, spoke softly in his faint, sweet Oklahoma accent. He always knew the details because Hazel briefed him well and he remembered it all because it was important to remember it all.

And now they were old, Charles was summoned more and more. He was a workhorse of condolence. The white shirts were always kept clean and the black suit at the ready, and it seemed they got it out every two weeks anymore.

The woman followed Charles to the cabin door in her wheelchair and turned him around one last time and smoothed his pocket flaps and sent him off. He moved slowly across the yard with his walking stick. He hollered at a boy and asked him to help him across the highway. Hazel leaned to watch him from the front window until he was out of sight.

They lived at the "Shady Grove," an archipelago of superannuated tourist cabins in Belle Fourche, South Dakota.

The cabins were arranged in two thoughtful, mirror-image crescent-rows beneath tall cottonwoods. Between the two crescents an erstwhile gravel driveway loop showed faintly through encroaching grass.

Across Highway 212 was a nearly identical set of cabins, the "Mountain View," in a similar magisterial grove. The two sets differed only in color; the cabins on the west side of the road were white, those on the east a cocoa brown. But they were all of 1920 vintage, small, nearly square clapboard structures inviting in scale and intention. They had prospered for three decades in their flickering cottonwood shade. Tourist families could walk from the cabins to the Belle Fourche and the Redwater rivers to fish.

Nowadays they sagged a bit. The brown and the white paints were shabby pintos. The red-shingle roofs were ratty in places and the eaves were full of twigs and leaves. Window screens were often torn and curling. Old drainpipes and rusty lawn tools and the occasional cast-off sink lay about the grounds.

The white world had abandoned the cabins years ago, but they were still weather-tight and they were still cozy in scale and pleasing as social architectural clusters. Most of them were inhabited, many by older people who had left the reservations, like Charles and Hazel, to find simple ease and good solid shade. A younger family or two were usually there as well; there were always children and grandchildren to stir the air and punctuate the midday naps. And the lines of the cabins softened now that there were people living in them full time.

Over the preceding decade the two clusters had taken on casual lineage affiliations as relatives heard of the places and their moderate rents. So the brown cabins tended toward a certain wide, loosely defined kin and their acquaintances, while the white cabins across the highway comprised more or less another.

In one cabin there lived an old silent man with one remaining incisor who worked in his yard carving cedar flutes that he sold to tourist shops. He continually smacked his lips as he worked, holding up the flute at arm's length, carefully sighting along it to keep it true.

Next to him lived a silent old man with a red nose, who covered all his windows with Rapid City newspapers and once a day crept down the three steps with his diamond-willow cane and circled the cabin one time and went back inside. Beside him dwelled an old half-Arikara man with a gray butch and one leg off at the knee; every weekend his daughter came and took him for a drive and ice cream.

There were old couples thankful for company, who kept their cabins neat and planted flowers by the stoops and small kitchen gardens in the rear and often sent food to the womanless men, and one large family with seven children that rented two cabins side by side to hold them all and stretched a canvas tarp between them for a breezeway. Formerly, they could be seen on Sunday mornings walking out the drive and filing north at the highway toward the Catholic church. Then one day the Catholic father told them the kids must have new shoes to go with their school uniforms. Now they turn south Sunday mornings toward the Episcopal services.

There was a middle-aged couple who made painted dance shawls for powwows and a single woman with children who taught at a local kindergarten. There was a part-time auto mechanic and a night janitor and a café cook.

In the summer people came and went, took trips to visit family and fairs. Some weeks the cabins bulged with guests and there were new teenagers whispering at night along the rivers. Winters, there was the low talk and the hunching, the football on television, the long sitting with the inner dailiness, and cautious walks across the snowy yard to see the neighbors. The little colony had the rough harmonious weave of any enclave; the insular hum and percolation. It strengthened and grew and after a few years it was as if the white town existed around the cabin colony to sell it beef and candy and white bread. 212 was like a river through it.

In the midst, Hazel was the busy archivist of woof and warp and due. She could catalog bloodlines and clancharacter with the best of them and chant it like Homer. She clarified things for the colony, she kept track. Warm days, she watched it all from her front yard. During the depths of winter she beaded earrings for her grandchildren and hooked rugs. She tended the gas heater beneath a photograph of a meadowlark torn from a magazine and watched it all from her window. When Charles brought in a particularly graphic, risqué parsnip from his snowy little root plot—a mandrakelike parsnip with two legs and a prominent male member—Hazel would laugh and clean it up, wrap it discreetly in newspaper and send it by child messenger to one of her women friends across the road. Later they would see each other across the way and wave little knowing waves and snicker like schoolgirls.

And Charles stabilized the cabins with his gentle humor and sweet diplomacy. He loved the children of the colony. He called one of them to him every evening and Sunday afternoons to read the comic pages aloud to him and de-

scribe the goings-on frame by frame, while he sat chuckling
and nodding. On good days he would call the child back for
a second reading an hour later.

He performed his funereal duties with a fluency that continually surprised himself. He was good at it; people liked to
see him coming up the road. As a young man he had been
skittish of that sort of thing; as a boy he had fled to the hills
along the Canadian River near Watonga, Oklahoma, to avoid
a funeral, and sat all the afternoon smoking in a hackberry
tree.

But he learned. In the past five years he had been called
all over the western Dakotas; twice to Riverton, Wyoming;
and once each to Sheridan, Billings, and Colorado Springs.
Everywhere he stood tall and half-blind and his words were
soft and soothing. He learned, laboriously, like a heavy bird
taking off from the ground. He always bore the pall left-side
middle so as not to stumble and fall.

Lately when called to Rapid City he had taken to having
a fancy cigar on the street in front of the big hotel and often
managed to work in an evening at the dog track, where he
sat quietly gazing at his shoes and stroking his salami nose,
enjoying the ebb and slow crescendo of the crowd as the
packs sailed from far-side to homestretch. He learned to take
pleasure from his duties, an honest, ambassadorial pleasure
that he considered a healthy by-product of all the sympathy
and sad suction and demanding protocol of departure. He
learned that what had at first seemed like the handling of
tarantulas was more like a juggling of bluebird chicks. He
observed it all with humble curiosity and an occasional anti-
Rosicrucian chuckle, as every two weeks or so they took the
black suit down from the closet while Hazel briefed him and

off he would go. Sometimes across the highway; sometimes catching a ride to Pine Ridge, or to Thunder Butte in the rain. A Minniconjou man run over by a locomotive. A young bull rider trampled in Cheyenne. An Oglala boy killed in Asia and that long, high, invisible flight back to South Dakota. An invaluable old woman who "slept away" on Pass Creek at noon on the Fourth of July.

◈

THERE were breakthroughs from the cabin dailiness. There were visitations and uplifts, bracing verticalities in a part of South Dakota where they were scarce and sorely needed.

There was a gifted twelve-year-old boy over in the Mountain Views, a boy who picked up distant conversations via birds of prey. Walking alone beside the Redwater or from the railroad bridge abutment nearby, he gazed off into the distance and waited. Sooner or later a soaring bird would come into conjunction with a car or an isolated house many miles south and the boy would hear the talk going on in there. Eagles brought him the important transmissions: messages of vague origin and ropy, private innuendo. Hawks, and even crows, those birds that follow highways in search of carrion, sent him lesser news and ranker gossip as they went their crooked ways.

The boy picked up sweat-stained trucker talk and random lovers' whispers from the bottomlands. From the reservations off to the south and east he pulled in a spotty flow of everyday news that he passed along to the cabin people. When the Swainson's hawks soared he heard breakfast chat from out near Faith or Redowl, and crowded-car conversations from along the Hermosa road. And very rarely, a deep, slow, eagle-relayed voice from somewhere over the wilder Black Hills.

And there was Elmer Foot, the old man who just died across the highway. He started something vertical once, a few years back. One night he was awakened by a disturbance in the garbage cans behind his cabin. Elmer got up and went to see about it. There, half in and half out of the streetlight, was a man rummaging through the trash. When Elmer spoke, the man straightened and turned to face him, tall, calm, and chiaroscuro. It was, Elmer said the next morning, the Lord.

A week later an elderly woman from the white cabins was walking home after dark with a loaf of bread. As she crossed the old bridge she saw a man sleeping on the ground, up under the abutment. She was startled and tried to tiptoe by, but the man rolled over and sat up. It was the Lord again, and he lifted one shapely hand and said to the woman, "Storms never last."

After that the cabin people were on the alert. They looked two and three times at strangers passing by that summer, and eyed the spry hoboes sunning by the rivers. No one was taken for granted; there were half-heard voices in the night and ghostly brushes with the Lord on both sides of the road. Charles chuckled and said, "I believe he's gone and moved into this neighborhood."

Cabin people appeared and disappeared over the years and countless scroungy lapdogs perished on the busy highway, but it was the gradual foothold and sunflowering of the colony that caught the hawk's eye, that the residents came and went by and looked up to as if it were in the treetops: the slow accretion of the social reef and its happenstance bivalve symmetry. Girls from the brown cabins married boys from the white. A girl swelled with child in the Shady Grove and people glanced slyly across the highway to the Mountain View. Given several generations, two dialects might well spring up in the camps, gently enforced by the highway-river.

And the seasons soared higher and higher now that people lived in them full-time, bent and hid and slept in them. Months mattered more than days; years more than months; and the sunflowering more than any single tale or thing.

Try as you may, Charles thought, it is in the treetops; it is always the no-one-man that steps forward from the choke-cherry patch.

❧

AND there was another fine autumn Saturday showed up like a moon—a big full day to look twice at. The first golden cottonwood leaves twirled down on the cabin roofs. The day was almost the color of those leaves. Wild turkey feathers lay scattered about the grove and tumbled lazily when a breeze hit them. People moved about slowly, hesitantly, like the cool-stunned yellow jackets thudding all day against screen doors as if they were drugged or happy beyond good sense.

Charles was napping in the bedroom with the radio down low. His long narrow shoes stood up like mule deer ears at the foot of the bed. Hazel sat in her wheelchair sorting rags for rugs. A tricycle creaked steadily from a yard down the way. The old man with one incisor sat by his steps in the sun, finishing a cedar flute. Every few minutes he blew a long mellow note to test the tone. *Thud, thud*—yellow jackets against a screen. . . .

Beyond the highway, the boy who heard from birds came back from a walk along the river and made a peanut butter and jelly sandwich while he told his mother some news. He told it in short robin-like phrases, each almost like a question: an old lady named Agnes Other Side was near death down on the reservation.

The boy's mother turned her boiling potatoes down low and put on her jacket and went out and across the yard. As she stood at the highway waiting for traffic to pass, Hazel saw her from her window. The old lady stirred and hoisted herself in her wheelchair. She strained and squinted so that her lips pulled back from her teeth.

She thought as she watched the woman crossing the road: "Who is it now? Maybe Rachel's brother's boy—he's been real sick down at Porcupine."

The old man across the yard blew a single, hollow thrush-note on his flute. Then Hazel twisted in her chair and called over her bony-thin shoulder: "Charles! Charles, wake up!"

THOUSAND LEGGERN

SHE grew up in the Yakima valley of Washington in a house immediately downwind from the big mint farms lining the river: a benevolent site that instilled in her early on a simple sense of the good life as one of regular, uplifting fragrance. Miles and decades after, she dismissed, with a firm, exile's superiority, the bouquet of the Dakota pines, when the wind was that way. Even the lubricative aroma of fresh-cut hay on August evenings bore no comparison to her ultimate touchstone: mint fields after an arousing rain.

She often taxied me around the Flicker country when I was carless and she usually worked the Yakima valley somewhere into our day-talk; it was an emerald kite above a hard flat life. Today she was driving me out to see Oscar Whitetail at his home far up on Bear-in-Lodge Creek. He had promised to take me out one day to find tree mushrooms. The woman knew the territory well and told me stories in a staccato monotone as we drove, her eyes moving methodically from highway to speedometer to rearview mirror. She nodded toward a battered concrete shell of a building standing a hundred yards off the road.

"Fireworks plant. Someone screwed up every five years or so and the place would blow all to hell. . . . There must have been a dozen men blown to bits at that place. One or two every five years. Someone slipped up for a split second and *bang*—that's the last of them. They finally gave up and closed the place a few years ago."

Beyond the thick-walled bunker relic I could see dust clouds where a herd of horses rolled in a good bare spot near the river.

We left the paved road after half an hour and drove back a series of tough gumbo tracks that rose and fell across the pine-speckled hills. One moment we were topping a grassy ridge and admiring the white bluffs twenty miles to the south. The next we were rocking through a deep draw where ash and box elder trees thrived. I saw the heavy, half-green scent of chokecherry blow turn the woman's head for an instant as we rumbled by.

Oscar was sitting quietly against a tree when we drove into his place. He got to his feet when he recognized us and waved us in, but soon lost interest. It was the only time I had ever seen him drunk.

We went inside the house with Oscar's wife and sat at the table talking and sipping sweet coffee. The old woman bore homemade tattoos on her hands and forearms: anachronistic boys' names in the bay at the base of the thumbs; L-O-V-E spaced across the lower knuckles of one hand, pricked in with a safety pin fifty years ago on a summer night. On her thin arms the ink-blue initials and arabesques were distended and fuzzed by the years like amorous old carvings on aspen bark.

She was tending a large cast-iron skillet full of curly thick-cut bacon and boiling a pot of corn mush on the stove. She told us shyly that Oscar was drunk for the first time since she had known him. Something had hit him and he went out and bought a bottle the night before. Now it was gone. We could see the lean dogs of the place gathered outside, rearing, maneuvering windward with their noses high, working to catch the bacon wafts.

Oscar came in while we chatted there. He approached me noncommittally, squinting a little. He lay his calm broad hand on my shoulder and spoke in a husky whisper: "I know you're FBI. I know damn well you're FBI." A moment later, while he stood waving gently like a tall pine beside the table, he bent again and said, to balance the intricate human equation, "But I love you, I love you." Then he went out to his tree.

I would come back another day and we would all walk easily through the stream bottoms looking for tree mushrooms in the box elder groves, talking softly, dropping the mushrooms into brown grocery bags.

❖

THE woman from the mint country drove me back to town. When we passed a rural arbor where dances and celebrations were held, she told me a powwow story. Some years ago she guided an elderly professor to the annual July get-together at this place. The old gentleman had spent his entire life comparing various marginal modes of subsistence on the North American continent: migrant cherry pickers in Michigan orchards; Baffin Island seabird egg gatherers; Louisiana nutria men. . . .

He was passing through the Flicker River region and the

woman agreed to escort him to this small *wacipi* for a look. They pulled in at midmorning and sat in their lawn chairs under the pine-bough arbor, fanning themselves with wide-brimmed hats, waiting for the dancing to begin.

By noon it had reached 100 degrees, bone-dry and droning. The professor flagged. The dancing had not begun. They told him "One o'clock sharp." He wet his handkerchief and mopped his face and head. At one-thirty he walked to the announcer's booth and inquired again, a bit testily this time, what was the holdup, what was the holdup exactly.

The woman from Washington calmed him, poured him lemonade, and taught him a hot-weather trick of the old Indian ladies—placing his wet, folded kerchief squarely on top of his balding head and leaving it there to cool the pate. That, with its ethnological overtones, held him until two-thirty. The naming ceremonies and the family giveaways dragged on.

At three-fifteen, still no dancing. He began to redden and rave, pacing behind his chair, throwing his arms about, raising his voice. The woman reached to soothe him, but it was too late. He broke away and stormed the announcer's booth with shouts of rage and indignation. He pointed at his watch and pounded on the wall. It was a terrible outburst that had the crowd on its feet, craning; vindictive, heavily educated spleen slashing at the salvationary roots of the host culture.

The woman and the Fox Society men finally gathered him up and put him in her long white car with a dowsing of cold water. Then she drove him, eyes closed and muttering, back to his motel in town.

And now she dropped me at my bicycle chained to a Chinese elm in the same hot town—merchants peeked from their murky windows—and I pedaled slowly out of the village and up into the cool pine-ridge haven just south. I made a quick camp and lay beneath an aromatic ponderosa until sundown, reading and gazing out over the long shimmering plain with a tiny jitterbug of badland on the skyline. But each time I looked too long I began seeing little groups of men being blown up into the air and down in a thousand smithereen confetti, men exploding from the earth like dusty geysers. . . .

That night I dreamt I was riding down the Flicker highway and came to a rural mailbox (an actual, waking-world mailbox I have passed many times), its name in bright gold letters: DVOŘÁK. But this time I wheeled the bike into the lane and took off for it, pedaling hard, soon hitting a steep pastoral downhill that I shot, faster and faster with the grade, the naturally suspected "Dvořák music" now faintly audible from up ahead (wild wind in my face, my mind flashing "First white man to ever set foot in these parts!"), then louder, full-symphonic as I zoomed in around a meadow curve to behold the shady ranch house, the mythic music blaring, radiating from the grove like sunlight off windows, and the Dvořáks lined up out front, shading their eyes and waving.